THE
SECRET
OF THE
SHELTER

By Hugh Morrison

MONTPELIER PUBLISHING
2021

Published in Great Britain by Montpelier Publishing.

ISBN: 9798718882582

Chapter One
The New House

'Here it is,' said Mr Thomas, as he slowed the car down. 'Our new home. Or to be precise, number 37, Cotswold Gardens, Northgate, London NW12 7GQ.'

James Thomas was always precise; he worked in a bank and so he had to be very careful about numbers and what order they came in. He carried over this habit into his home life, such as now, when the family was moving house. He carefully eased the car from the tree-lined road onto the driveway of the house, and switched off the engine.

'What do you think then?' he said, turning to his wife, Claire, beside him in the passenger seat, and his son, Jack, who was sitting in the back. Jack, who was eleven, kicked the back of his father's seat out of boredom.

'Don't do that, please,' said Mr Thomas. 'I said what do you think about the new house?'

'Well I've seen it before, when we viewed it,' said Mrs Thomas. 'What about you, Jack?' She turned to her son, who was now peering out of the window at the house. It looked to him like just another ordinary, boring London house in a road full of similar ones.

'It looks a bit small,' said Jack.

'Ah but that's an illusion,' said Mr Thomas. 'It's like Dr Who's Tardis on TV. It looks small on the outside, but on the inside it's enormous.'

'Really?' asked Jack. He was sometimes not sure if his father was teasing him or not.

'Of course not, don't be ridiculous,' said Mr Thomas with a laugh. 'There's no such thing as a Tardis.'

'So it is just a small, ordinary house,' said Jack.

'Well, people were smaller in the old days when it was built,' said Mr Thomas. 'They didn't sit around getting fat from eating too much McDonalds and playing on their tablets all day, like you.'

Mr Thomas was always saying things like that to Jack. He believed in Fresh Air and Exercise. Jack wasn't fat; in fact he was sometimes teased at school for being skinny and a bit small, and having slightly curly reddish hair, but he did like McDonalds and he did prefer playing computer games to going out.

'Dad's just teasing,' said Mrs Thomas. 'The house isn't really that old. Certainly less than a hundred years ago. When was it built – 1930?'

'1934, to be precise,' said Mr Thomas.

'Well I think that's old,' said Jack.

'It's not as old as the house we've just left,' said Mrs Thomas. 'That was built in 1870, and you kept saying you didn't want to leave that one.'

'Yes,' said Jack. 'But our old house was different. It was a *proper* old house with corridors and a cellar, and a big garden. This one's just old and ordinary.'

'That should suit me and your mother just fine then,' said Mr Thomas with a chuckle.

'Speak for yourself,' said Mrs Thomas, digging her husband in the ribs. 'Anyway, our old house was far too big for just the three of us,' she said, in a slightly sad voice. Then she quickly cheered up. 'Come on Jack,' she said, 'let's have a look around.'

They got out of the car into the warm summer sunshine. There was a sound of lawnmowers in the distance, and then a clattering, rattling sound from the end of the street.

'That's the railway,' said Mr Thomas. 'The tube trains run right past the end of the street, and the station is only a couple of minutes' walk away. It's one of the main reasons I chose this place – I'll be able to get into work almost as quickly as I could from Hampstead, even though we're further out from the City here.'

Jack looked towards the end of the street and saw a long railway bridge, with a red tube train rattling along it. He liked the idea of being able to see a railway from the house. That was, at least, something they didn't have in their old house, because in that part of London the nearest railway ran underground.

Mr and Mrs Thomas began to unpack the bags from the boot of the car. Jack looked at the small front garden of the house, which contained only a few small bushes and a patch of lawn, most of which seemed to have died and gone brown in the sun. He looked up at the house; it looked just as boring, he thought, from the garden as it had looked from the car. It had a boring white front door, boring white walls and three boring windows. Jack sighed and hoped that at least he'd be able to see the railway from his room.

Then Jack noticed the house next door. Not on the left side of the house – that was just another boring London house like this one – but on the other side, the last house before the railway line. There was something different about this house.

It was not painted white like most of the houses in the street, but it was a sort of dirty brown colour. The windows were different as well; they did not have the modern white plastic frames that most houses have, but instead it had the old wooden type of frame, painted in a yellowish colour, although most of the paint seemed to have peeled off them.

Jack noticed that some of the windows were cracked, and one of the little ones at the top of the house was completely broken, as if someone had thrown a stone at it. All the windows had thick, stained curtains pulled across them, so that it was impossible to see anything inside.

The yellow paint on the door had peeled off as well, leaving bare wood showing underneath. There was a little window in the door made of coloured glass in the pattern of a sailing ship; part of it was mended with sticky tape. The front garden was almost like a jungle, with bramble bushes and long weeds everywhere, which extended around the side of the house and crept up its walls.

Jack's mouth felt dry and he swallowed. The house looked a bit creepy. Were they moving next door to a haunted house?, he wondered.

'Come on Jack, get a move on,' said Mr Thomas, as he pushed open the front door of their house with his elbow. 'Give me a hand with some of these bags, then you can choose your room.'

Jack walked into the hallway and was not surprised to find that the house looked just as dull inside as it did outside. The walls and carpets were all the same cream colour; there was a small kitchen and a big combined sitting room and dining room. A modern sliding door opened out onto the back garden, which he could see was just an empty expanse of lawn with a hedge and small shed at the bottom.

The ground floor of the house was packed with wooden crates and boxes that the removal men had left there. Some of the furniture from their old house was also there, but a lot of it had to be sold, because Mr Thomas said there wasn't enough room for it at the new house.

Jack looked in a few boxes and then breathed a sigh of relief when he found the one in which he had packed all his stuff, including his tablet. Mr Thomas began checking off items in the boxes carefully against a list printed on a sheet of paper.

'Come and have a look upstairs, Jack,' said Mrs Thomas.

She led the way up the staircase to the first floor, where there was a landing with several doors off it. She began opening the doors. 'This is the bathroom – not much to write home about really – this is the main bedroom – what they call the master bedroom – Dad and I will sleep there. I thought that this one here,' – she indicated a slightly smaller room next to the master bedroom – 'could be my studio.'

Mrs Thomas was an artist, who drew and painted pictures for children's books, and so was able to work from home.

'You can choose one of these rooms,' she said, pointing to two more doors at the end of the corridor. 'I expect you'll like this one, as it's bigger.' She showed Jack a fairly large bedroom with fitted cupboards with a view of the back garden and the houses beyond. Jack looked around briefly and noted the view. 'Can I see the other one?' he asked.

'Of course,' said Mrs Thomas. 'It's a bit poky though. It's what they used to call a box-room I think.' She opened the door to reveal a rather small room, with a little fireplace in the corner with shelves next to it. Through the window, Jack could see part of the old, creepy house next door. It looked even more creepy from this side. Beyond it, he could see the railway bridge. Suddenly there was a flash of light and a rattling noise as a tube train rushed across the bridge.

'I prefer this one,' said Jack.

'Are you sure?' said Mrs Thomas. 'I wouldn't want the trains to wake you up in the night.'

'They won't, mum,' said Jack.

'And all you've got to look at is that eyesore next door. I do hope someone buys it and does the place up.'

'Doesn't anybody live there?'

'I don't think so, it looks abandoned. The estate agent – that's the man who showed us round the house – said he wasn't sure if anybody still lived there. Still, I suppose I shouldn't complain. Dad mentioned the bad state of the place next door, and the seller agreed to drop the price.'

'Why?'

'I suppose he thought it lowers the tone.'

'What does that mean?'

Mrs Thomas laughed. 'It's something snobbish people say when there's something ugly next door. I don't think Dad's that much of a snob really, I think he was just trying to save some money.'

Jack looked out of the window at the side of the back garden next door. It looked like a thick, dark jungle, even though it was daylight and the sun was shining. Another tube train shot across the bridge, this time going in the opposite direction – he could even see people sitting in the carriages, reading newspapers. He decided he was going to like this room.

'Remember your cousin Ella from America is coming next week to stay,' said Mrs Thomas. 'So she'll have the other room. Last chance to change your mind.'

Jack had forgotten that his cousin was coming. But he was sure he'd rather be able to see the creepy old house from his room than she would.

'It's OK, mum,' he said. 'This room's fine. If I don't like it I can always change after Ella's left.'

'Alright then. Now you start unpacking your stuff and I'll make us all something to eat.'

The following day was Sunday, and by late afternoon, Mr Thomas decided he had had enough of unpacking boxes, putting up pictures and moving furniture around. The house had finally started to look habitable, and he decided that it was time for Fresh Air and Exercise.

'Come on, Jack,' said Mr Thomas. 'It's time we got outside for a bit. Shame to waste the last of the sun. Let's go for a bike ride, have a look round the new area.'

Jack had just about finished unpacking his toys and books and arranging things on the shelves by the fireplace in his room. He was looking forward to catching up on his computer games, but Mr Thomas was insistent.

'I'll show you the sights of Northgate, and how to find your way around,' he said, as he wheeled their bikes out from the side gate into the front garden. Mrs Thomas declined to come out, as she had a lot of drawings to do for a new book.

Mr Thomas walked his bicycle alongside Jack while he cycled slowly along the pavement. He wasn't allowed to ride on the road until he'd done his Bikeability test, and that wasn't until next term.

'Are we going to the Heath?' asked Jack.

'Sorry, no,' said Mr Thomas. 'Hampstead Heath is miles away from here. Maybe when you're older we'll attempt it, but for now we'll have to make do with a few turns around Northgate Recreation Ground.'

The reached the recreation ground, and Jack's heart sank. When they lived at their old house, every Saturday he and his father had cycled around Hampstead Heath, a huge area of parkland and woods, filled with paths and trails and even a sort of ruined temple, that Mr Thomas said was called a folly. Northgate Recreation Ground, by contrast, was just a big open space with grass, some football goalposts and a cycle path running around the edge.

As they cycled around the park, Mr Thomas pointed things out to Jack. 'There's the public library,' he said, indicating a large modern glass building, 'and that's the old police station,' he said, pointing at a red-brick building with a blue lamp outside. 'I think it's been turned into flats now, though,' he said. 'Oh and look,' he added. 'There's the tube station.'

Jack looked on the other side of the park to see a long, low railway bridge. There was a small building next to it, made of white tiles, with the words 'Northgate Park' and 'London Underground' painted in blue above the door.

'Why does it say "Underground" when it's not underground?' asked Jack.

'Well most of the line is underground,' said Mr Thomas, 'but towards the end of the line, it comes out of the tunnel, where you can see it. If you ever get lost around here, look for the tube line. See where it runs up the hill there? That's the bridge that goes past our house. So you can always follow the railway line home.'

'Oh yeah,' said Jack. He wondered why he should ever get lost, though. His parents took him everywhere because he wasn't allowed out on his own until he was in secondary school.

They stopped for a rest on a bench, and looked out

at the park as the shadows lengthened in the evening sun. It all looked very different to their old home, thought Jack. Everything seemed smaller and newer here.

'Dad,' said Jack, after a pause. 'Are we poor?'

Mr Thomas laughed. 'What on earth do you mean?'

'Freddy at school said I had to leave because I was poor, and that you couldn't afford to pay the school.'

'Do you mean Freddy Marchant?'

'Yes.'

'I thought so. I play, or rather I played, golf with his father sometimes and we talk about work. I mentioned to him that we were downsizing, and he must have told Freddy.'

'What does downsizing mean?'

'It means having a bit of a smaller house because you don't need such a big one. The old house was too big for us and was costing a lot of money to run.'

'But why did that mean I had to leave school?' asked Jack. 'I liked it at St Edmund's.'

'Well, that's another part of the downsizing. It was costing a lot of money to keep you at St Edmund's. You're old enough to start secondary school after this summer, so it was a good time to get you a place in a school out here in Northgate.'

'Why here though?'

'Because the schools in this part of London are quite good and, what's more, they're free. There aren't many good free ones where we used to live. You know that I lost my job and it took quite a long time to get another one. Well, I don't get paid as much at my new job, and Mum's work is unpredictable, so we had to find ways to save money.'

Jack's face flushed red and he suddenly felt angry. 'So we *are* poor,' he said.

'Don't be silly, Jack,' said Mr Thomas. 'Being poor means not having enough to eat, or not having a roof over your head. We've got absolutely nothing to worry about and we're far better off than most people on this planet.'

'I suppose so…' said Jack.

'Good,' said Mr Thomas. 'Now, speaking of having enough to eat, I don't believe I've showed you where the McDonalds is around here.'

'Is there one?' said Jack, brightening up.

'Indeed there is,' said Mr Thomas, 'and your poor, destitute father is willing to spend his last few coppers on a Big Mac, just for you.'

That night, as Jack got into bed for the first time in the new house, he looked out of his bedroom window before drawing the curtains. It was nearly dark outside, and although he could see lights on in other houses further away, the house next door looked completely black. He was pretty sure that nobody could be living there. Then, just as he was about to draw the curtains, he thought he saw a flicker of light from the upstairs bedroom, as if someone was shining a torch around.

He looked again but couldn't see anything, and then, through the open window, heard the now familiar rattling sound of a tube train crossing the bridge. He noticed that the lights from the carriage

11

were reflected in the darkened windows of the house next door. Was that what he had seen just now? But the tube train hadn't passed the bridge when he saw the light in the upstairs window.

Was somebody in the house?, he wondered. He decided he had probably just seen the reflected light from the train, but to be on the safe side, he shut the bedroom window and locked it before going to sleep.

Chapter Two
Cousin Ella from America

'Why are we going on the tube train to the airport?' asked Jack, as they waited on the platform of Northgate Park underground station. 'Couldn't we go by car?'

'It's much easier by tube,' said Mrs Thomas. 'There's an awful lot of traffic around the airport and you have to pay quite a lot for parking. But the train goes right there.' She pointed at the map of the railway network on the wall behind them, and traced the line they were on all the way to the airport station. 'See,' she said. 'We don't even have to change lines.'

After a couple of minutes' wait, a train arrived and they got on. As it was the middle of the day, the train was nearly empty and they were able to find seats easily.

As the train left the platform, Jack watched through the window at the seemingly endless rows of houses along the railway line. They all looked much the same, until suddenly he saw one that stood out from the others because of its dark, stained walls.

'Look!' said Jack. 'That's the creepy house. The one next to ours, I mean.'

'Oh, I must have missed it,' said Mrs Thomas, looking up from her paperback book. 'The line does run much closer to our house than I thought. The trains have been waking me up in the morning. Dad says it's a useful alarm clock.'

After what seemed a very long time, they finally arrived at the airport and Mrs Thomas guided Jack through the busy terminal to a big glass gate where they sat down to wait for the passengers coming off the flight from New York.

Jack, who had been hoping to see some planes landing and taking off, was disappointed to find that the terminal building did not seem to have any windows; in fact, it looked to him more like a big shopping centre, and he always found shopping centres boring.

'Why aren't Auntie Paula and Uncle Marty coming this time?' asked Jack. 'They came last time.'

Auntie Paula was Mrs Thomas' younger sister, who had moved to the USA years before and married a man who, like Mr Thomas, worked in a bank. Jack remembered that a couple of years ago, they and their daughter Ella, his cousin, had all come to stay with them.

'Well,' said Mrs Thomas with some hesitation, 'it's rather expensive for them all to fly over. Uncle Marty's had some problems at work, like Dad has, and so they decided it would be better if Ella came on her own and stayed with us.'

Money problems again, thought Jack. It seemed to him that grown-ups worried about money most of the time.

A thought struck him. 'How come Ella's allowed to go on the plane on her own? She's only eleven, like me.'

'That's all organised by the airline,' said Mrs Thomas. 'They get one of the stewardesses to look after you and make sure you're alright. Oh, look, this must be her now.'

Jack looked up to see that the glass gates in front of them had opened. A crowd of people walked through and he noticed Ella, walking with a lady in a red uniform.

Ella was taller than Jack remembered. She had blonde hair tied back in a pony tail. She was wearing a purple hoodie with sparkly bits on it, pink leggings and purple trainers, and was pulling a purple suitcase behind her. He was looking forward to meeting her again, but couldn't help wishing he had a boy cousin instead. He'd never seen so much pink and purple on one person in his life.

Ella spotted them and called out. 'Aunt Claire!'
Mrs Thomas rushed over to her and they hugged each other. Jack didn't like hugging much, especially not girls, so he stood back a little and waved, while trying to look uninterested.

'Hey Jack,' said Ella, and waved at him. Jack remembered from TV programmes that Americans always seemed to say 'hey' when they meant 'hi.'

Mrs Thomas had to sign a form and then the red-uniformed stewardess said 'Goodbye Ella, have a great trip.'

Then the two of them hugged. There seemed to be a bit too much hugging going on today, thought Jack.

Lots of people around him were doing it as well, so he folded his arms to make it clear he didn't want it done to him.

A few minutes later, while they waited on the platform for the tube train, Ella pulled out a shiny phone with a pink case from the pocket of her hoodie. 'Look at my new phone, Jack. Isn't it cool? Dad said it will work over here, too, so I'll be able to keep in touch with them and with you as well. What's your number?'

Jack didn't want to have to tell Ella that he wasn't allowed a phone until he was at secondary school. Mr Thomas had said that before then, it was a pointless waste of money and that he'd probably end up dropping it down the toilet by accident anyway.

'Er, I'm between phones at the moment,' said Jack, trying to sound grown up.

'When will you get your new one?' said Ella.

'Erm…it's on order. Sometime soon, I think,' said Jack.

'Oh,' said Ella. 'Well never mind. I just thought it would be cool for us to message each other if we're a long way apart in the house. Your house is pretty big, isn't it?'

'Erm, kind of,' said Jack. 'But we've moved. Our new house is a bit smaller than the old one.'

'That's a shame,' said Ella. 'Your other house was neat, next to those woods.'

Jack felt a tinge of sadness at having their old house, and suddenly felt the need to impress Ella.

'The new house is right next to a haunted house.'

Ella gave him a pitiful look. The attempt to impress

her did not seem to have worked.

'Seriously?' snorted Ella. 'Come on Jack, how old are you? Ghosts aren't real. You only get haunted houses in stories.'

'Well it's definitely creepy, and last night I saw someone moving around in one of the rooms.'

Ella pretended to be scared, and put both her hands up to her face. 'Ooh, someone was moving around in a room, it must be a ghost, Dear Lord, someone save me!' Then she burst out laughing. Jack felt his face turn red. He was relieved when he saw the tube train stop in front of them.

Ella punched him lightly on the shoulder as they got on the train. 'It's OK Jack, I'm only teasing. Come on, I'll show you some of my phone games while I send a text to my mom and dad to tell them I've arrived.'

Ella and Mrs Thomas talked quite a lot on the tube on the way back home. Ella, thought Jack, seemed to think everything in London that she saw from the train was either 'totally cute' or 'totally awesome'. Jack noticed that small things she saw, such as a red pillar box or an old Mini car, the kind that Mr Bean had in those old comedy videos, were 'cute', and big things, like the River Thames and the large metal bridge that they crossed over it on, were 'awesome'.

Jack wasn't quite sure why a post box and a car were so worthy of attention. Anyway, he thought, at least Ella didn't seem to be a show off, like some of the girls he knew from school. He hoped that they would get along, even though they probably wouldn't be best friends, because she was a girl.

As they walked from Northgate Park tube station to the house, Jack felt a bit embarrassed because not only was he walking with his mother, which was bad enough, but also, she had made him pull Ella's big suitcase along behind him. Not only was the suitcase bright purple, it also had some sort of glitter on it, and very noisy wheels. Jack was worried that somebody from school might notice him. He relaxed a bit when he remembered that nobody from his school lived around here, and anyway, he wouldn't be going back there next term.

'This is so cute!' said Ella as Mrs Thomas opened the front door of the house. Jack watched Ella to see if she would notice the creepy old house next door. She gave it a quick glance but didn't seem to pay it much attention and carried on chatting to Mrs Thomas, as Jack struggled to lift the purple suitcase over the doorstep.

'It's a little bit smaller than our old house,' said Mrs Thomas, 'and I'm afraid we don't have all that lovely heath on our doorstep.'

'That's a shame,' said Ella. 'That was awesome.'

There she goes again, thought Jack. Everything was either cute or awesome for Ella.

'I'll show you to your room, and then we can all have something to eat,' said Mrs Thomas.

She took Ella's case and carried it upstairs, as she said it was too heavy for Jack to manage on his own.

'Thanks for wheeling my case from the subway,' said Ella as they followed Mrs Thomas up the stairs.

Jack blushed, and wondered whether any boys living in the street he might later become friends with had seen him with the embarrassing purple monstrosity. He hadn't seen any other children outside, so he decided he was probably safe enough.

'That's OK,' said Jack. 'But what do you mean, the subway? I thought a subway was a sort of road crossing.'

'The subway's what they call the tube in New York,' said Mrs Thomas, as she rounded the top of the staircase. 'Right Ella?'

Ella frowned. 'You're right. I guess I'd better get used to calling it the tube. Although back home that's what my dad calls the TV.'

'You were probably a bit too young to notice all these little differences last time you came,' said Mrs Thomas. 'But don't worry, you'll get used to it. Now,' she said, opening the door of the back bedroom,' here's your room.'

'Oh it's…incredible!' said Ella. 'I love it.'

Jack was relieved that she didn't call it cute.

'And you've got a really cute back yard,' she said, looking through the window.

'We call it a garden rather than a yard,' said Mrs Thomas, 'but yes, it will certainly be a bit easier to manage than the one at our old house. And we won't need to have a gardener coming in either, as I've decided Jack here is going to be our new gardener.'

Mrs Thomas pulled Jack close to her and ruffled his hair. He found it highly embarrassing to have to put up with that in front of his cousin, and he wriggled to get free.

'But I don't know anything about gardening,' said Jack. 'That's for grown-ups, isn't it?'

'Don't worry,' said Mrs Thomas. 'I don't mean a real gardener, like the one that used to come to us at our old house. All you need to do is mow the lawn and dig over the flowerbeds, and perhaps I'll show you how to grow some seeds and plants if I have time. Does that sound good?'

Jack looked doubtful. 'Dad says he'll pay you,' said Mrs Thomas.

'OK,' said Jack. 'How much?'

Mrs Thomas laughed. 'Well, he's the one who works in a bank. You'll have to ask him.'

'That sounds neat,' said Ella, who was unpacking her clothes from the purple suitcase and laying them neatly on the bed. 'Can I help Jack with the garden too?'

'If you really want to,' said Mrs Thomas. 'But you don't have to. Wouldn't you rather see all the sights of London, like Big Ben, and Buckingham Palace, and the London Eye?'

'Not really,' said Ella, who was pushing out the creases on her clothes. Jack noticed nearly everything in her suitcase was either pink, purple, turquoise or had glitter of some sort on it. 'I remember going to all those places last time I came here. I think this time I'd like to just chill.'

'Well…' said Mrs Thomas doubtfully. 'I do think we ought to go to at least one or two places. It is part of your education, after all. But that said, I do have quite a lot of work on at the moment, and your Uncle James is out at work all day, so we can't really have big trips out all the time anyway. We'll do something at the weekend, how about that?'

'Fine,' said Ella with a shrug. 'I'll probably just message with my friends and chill in the back yard, I mean, the back garden.'

'I thought you were going to help me do my gardening,' said Jack.

'Oh sure,' said Ella with a smile. 'That too.'

'Well,' said Mrs Thomas, 'I'll get us all something to eat. Maybe Jack can show you his room.'

'That would be awesome,' said Ella.

Jack showed Ella into his little room. 'What do you think?' he asked.

'It's kind of nice,' said Ella. 'Where's the creepy old house you told me about? The one you said was haunted.'

Ella laughed and Jack felt himself blush.

'It's right out there,' he said, pointing proudly through the window.

Ella got up on tiptoe to look out of the window, and frowned. 'Is that it? I saw that when we came in from the street. It doesn't look creepy to me. There's a house near us back home that's way more scary than that. Somebody got shot there, and the police put yellow tape over the door so that nobody could get inside.'

Jack felt embarrassed again. 'I'm pretty sure there was somebody creeping about in there though, with a torch.'

'Well I don't think it looks scary,' said Ella. 'I think it just looks kind of sad, like some old guy lives there who can't afford to paint his house. Or maybe a crazy person.'

Jack was disappointed that Ella didn't think the

house was scary, so he pointed out of the open window at its garden, which was a dense jungle of trees, creepers and high weeds which reached all the way to the house.

'But look at the garden,' urged Jack. 'It's like a little hidden forest. There could be anything in there, like, wild animals, or even a dead body.'

'Don't be stupid, it's just full of weeds,' said Ella. She took out her phone and began scrolling through her text messages.

'I bet you wouldn't go in there though,' said Jack.

'Of course not, why would I go into someone's house?' said Ella, as she began tapping out a text message.

Jack couldn't help wanting to get Ella's attention. He still felt the new house and garden was a bit too boring and that he ought, somehow, to impress her.

'I don't mean the house,' said Jack. 'We might get into really big trouble if we went in there. I mean the garden. There's a loose bit of the fence and we could easily get through. If anyone saw us we could say we were looking for a ball or something.'

Ella put her phone down and looked out of the window. Two of the planks of the fence were leaning at an angle, leaving a hole large enough for a child to squeeze through.

'Oh yeah,' she said. 'I see the gap. But I bet you're too scared to go in there.'

Jack suddenly wished he hadn't started all this. But it was too late to back down now. He swallowed hard.

'Alright, I'll go in. But only if you come as well.'

Jack hoped this would put Ella off and enable him to cancel the plan with some dignity intact. But it was not to be.

'Sure,' said Ella. 'I'm not scared of some crazy old senior's back yard. I'll climb through the fence with you. And just to show I'm not scared, I'll even go first.'

'OK but not right now,' said Jack. 'Supper will be ready soon and my dad will be home any minute. Then it will be too dark.'

'Sounds like you're chicken,' said Ella.

'I'm not,' replied Jack. 'We'll definitely go in tomorrow.'

'We'd better,' said Ella. 'Otherwise I'll tell all my friends back home that my cousin's a chicken.'

Ella laughed and Jack felt his face redden again. He looked out of the window at the overgrown garden next door and bit his lip.

'We'll definitely go in tomorrow, first thing,' he said. 'And *I'll* go first.'

Chapter Three
The Jungle Garden

The next day, the weather was a bit cloudy, and at breakfast Mrs Thomas suggested that if Jack and Ella wanted to start work on the garden, they ought to start early as it was probably going to rain later.

Mr Thomas had to leave early to catch the tube to work, but because Mrs Thomas worked from home she was able to spend a few minutes showing Jack and Ella around the garden before she got started.

She showed them the little wooden shed where the things like spades and flower pots were kept. Many of them were still in boxes from the move so Jack and Ella started unpacking them. Then Mrs Thomas showed them how to use the electric lawnmower.

'Gosh,' she said, looking at her watch. 'I've lost track of time. I've got a big drawing to do for a children's book today, and I'd better get started. If you need any help, just call me.'

'OK,' said Jack and Ella.

Once Mrs Thomas had definitely gone into the house, Jack started digging over one of the flowerbeds by the shed.

'Aren't you forgetting something?' said Ella, with a

smile. She pointed to the hole in the fence. Jack remembered that the dare was still to be carried out.

'But what if my mum sees us?' said Jack.

'But what if my mum sees us?' mimicked Ella, in a babyish version of Jack's voice. She then laughed and pointed towards the house. 'Look, there's all these bushes and stuff at the bottom of the garden, so I don't think she can see anything down here. And isn't her workroom on the other side of the house, anyway?

'I suppose so,' said Jack, as he kicked some of the soil in the flowerbed so that it made a little cloud of dust.

Ella folded her arms. 'I'm pretty sure you're too chicken,' she said.

'I'm not,' said Jack. 'Come on, let's get this over with.'

Jack swallowed hard and felt his heart pounding in his chest. He walked over to the fence and moved aside the two loose planks. Inside, all he could see was a sort of dark forest of weeds and brambles. Small insects were buzzing about and there was a musty smell in the air, like you get in old castles and churches.

Jack looked to his right to check that his mother wasn't looking from the house, and also that nobody was watching from the next-door house. The dark, dirty windows with their peeling frames looked down on him blankly, and he couldn't see any movement inside.

It was now or never, he thought, and squeezed through the gap in the fence into the jungle beyond.

He checked again to make sure nobody was watching from the house, expecting at any minute for some angry man to come rushing out of the back door, but the house remained silent.

He turned to Ella. 'Come on, you're supposed to come too,' he said.

Ella bit her lip and glanced briefly at the old house.

Now it was Jack's turn to do some teasing. 'If you don't come,' he said, 'I'll tell all *my* friends *you're* chicken'.

'Don't you dare,' said Ella. 'I'm coming. I was just checking your mom wasn't watching.'

'Shh!' said Jack. 'I don't think anyone can see us but they might hear us. We've got to whisper.'

'OK,' said Ella in a loud whisper. 'What do we do now?'

'Follow me,' said Jack. He crept slowly forward into the undergrowth, with Ella close behind. They could only move slowly, because there were so many branches around them, and some of them had thorns, so Jack had to push them back carefully without getting his hands scratched.

'Ugh,' said Ella. 'This place is full of bugs. I already felt one bite me.'

'Want to go back?' said Jack, hopefully.

'No!' said Ella. 'We've come this far, we might as well see if there's anything in here.'

'You mean, like dead bodies?' asked Jack.

'Don't be stupid,' said Ella. 'I mean stuff from the old days, like, I don't know, tools and stuff. Or maybe even an old car. That would be totally cool.'

'Here's something,' said Jack. He pulled at a rusty

bit of metal in the undergrowth. After some tugging, a metal frame with two wheels emerged. 'I think it's an old lawn-mower,' said Ella. 'From the times before they had electric ones. That's kind of cool, I guess.'

'Look at this!' said Jack. Next to the old lawnmower was a row of cracked and broken windows, with some large cracked plant pots behind them.

'It looks like an old greenhouse,' said Jack. 'My grandpa's got one a bit like this. He got annoyed once because I accidentally broke one of the windows when I was playing football near it.'

A sly smile crept over Ella's face. 'Well, if you like breaking windows Jack, now's your opportunity.'

'You mean smash one of these?' asked Jack, doubtfully. 'I don't think we should, it doesn't belong to us.'

'So what?' said Ella. 'The whole thing's pretty much broken anyways. '

'But what if someone hears?'

'They won't. Watch me.'

Ella picked up a stone from the ground and threw it at one of the panes of glass. There was a splintering sound and the whole pane fell in pieces onto the carpet of weeds below.

'Cool!' said Jack. 'Let me do one.'

Jack picked up an even bigger stone and hurled it at the last remaining unbroken pane of glass in the ruined greenhouse. It shattered with a loud tinkling sound.

'That was awesome,' said Ella.

'Shh!' said Jack. 'I think someone's coming!'

Ella looked horrified. 'I didn't hear anything!'

'Keep quiet,' whispered Jack. They both crouched down and kept quiet and still. Finally Jack stood up.

'I think it must have been someone in the street,' said Jack. 'Anyway, they can't see us. Let's go on a bit.'

He pushed ahead and plunged his arms into a thick hedge which was, as far as he could tell, near the bottom of the garden. With some effort he was able to pull the hedgerow apart and step through into a little clearing. It was then that he saw something.

'Wow!' said Jack. 'Look at this, Ella.'

'What is it?' said his cousin, looking over Jack's shoulder.

The two children looked at a squat little building with a curved metal roof. It was half buried in the ground and much of the roof was covered in soil and weeds, although one side of the roof looked as if it had been bashed in with an enormous hammer. There was a little flight of steps going down to a small doorway; inside, there seemed to be nothing but pitch black.

'What is that?' said Ella. 'Some kind of garden shed?'

'No,' said Jack. 'I think I know what this is. I've seen a picture of one. It's an air raid shelter.'

'No way,' said Ella, in disbelief. 'You mean, like, against missiles and stuff? That little thing?'

'I'm sure that's what it is,' said Jack, who walked closer to the little building. 'We did a project on the

Second World War in school. It started in 1939. Britain had a war with Germany.'

'America was in it too,' said Ella. 'We did this in school as well, for Veterans Day. It was kind of boring, though.'

'OK,' said Jack. 'I wasn't sure if America was in it or not. But Britain definitely was and lots of bombs got dropped on London. People used to get inside these shelters when bombs were falling.'

'You mean they had bombs and stuff in London in the World War Two times? I thought that was only in some place in Europe.'

'No, I think my teacher said there were bombs here in London too,' said Jack. 'There must have been, or else why did they build a shelter here?'

'I don't believe you,' said Ella. 'It's just some old shack, probably full of garbage.'

'Only one way to find out,' said Jack. He made his way carefully down the little steps, which were covered in weeds. He paused slightly in front of the little doorway. The musty smell was stronger here, and he cautiously looked round the edge of the entrance.

'Jack, be careful,' said Ella anxiously. 'There could be rats in there.' She noticed that the jungle-garden, already quite dark because of all the trees and brambles which cut out most of the light, had started to become darker. She looked up and saw that dark grey clouds had started to cover the sky.

'Come here Ella, there's some stuff in here,' whispered Jack loudly.

Ella walked over to the shelter and stood behind

Jack as he looked through the doorway. She was ready to run if anything really nasty, like rats, turned out to be in there.

'I'm going in,' said Jack, and before Ella could warn him further, he stepped down into the black hole of the entranceway. Ella had no choice but to follow him.

Inside, it wasn't as dark as the children had expected it to be; it was gloomy but not pitch black, and there was still enough light coming in from the doorway for them to see what was inside the shelter.

'It's really small,' said Ella. 'I thought it would be like a big underground base, or something.'

'No,' said Jack. 'I remember seeing a picture of one when we did it at school. They were just like a little bedroom really. Look, this must have been the bunk beds.'

Jack pointed to a rough wooden frame on one side of the room. It had a rusted metal mesh over it, and ivy had grown through a crack in the metal wall and twined itself round the leg of the bunk. Next to the bunk was an old crate and on top of it was a pile of objects that looked like old tins, covered in thick dust. Jack picked some of them up but he couldn't read any of the labels as they were so rusted over; but as he replaced them he noticed a strange looking black object next to them.

'Wow,' said Jack. 'Look, it's a gas mask.'

'What's that for?' said Ella.

'I'm not sure, I think people wore them in case they got hit by a bomb that had poison in it.'

'Oh,' said Ella.

Jack picked up the mask which had two big round eye-holes and a piece of round metal like a big salt shaker where someone's nose would go. The material crumbled in his hands and he put it back on the crate in case it got damaged.

'Pity I can't wear it,' he said.

'That would be gross,' said Ella. 'Hey look at this!'

Ella peered at an old, tattered, official looking poster which was peeling off the metal wall of the shelter. She couldn't make out all the words, as it was so faded, but she could see the largest lettering at the top and read it out to Jack.

'*London Borough of Northbridge. Your air raid precautions. What to do in an air raid.*'

'See,' said Jack. 'I was right. I told you this was an raid shelter.'

'OK,' said Ella. 'You were right. This is totally cool. It was a good find.'

'Is it getting darker?' asked Jack.

The gloom in the shelter had begun to deepen, and they could now barely make out each other's faces. They looked out of the doorway and saw that it was now almost as dark as night.

'We should go,' said Ella. 'I don't like it in here now, it's getting too dark. There's probably going to be a storm. And your mom will be wondering where we are.'

'She won't notice we've gone,' said Jack. 'I want to stay a bit longer. I…'

Just then there was a huge crash of thunder and a flash of light outside, and the shelter shook and rattled slightly.

'Wow,' said Jack. 'That was the loudest thunder I've ever heard!'

'Shh!' said Ella. 'I think I hear someone outside.'

'I don't hear…'

'Jack be quiet!' hissed Ella. Both children stood immobile by the doorway of the shelter, listening.

They both heard a man's voice in the far distance. It sounded like he was shouting, but they couldn't make out the words.

'Jack, we've got to go,' whispered Ella. 'What if there is some crazy old guy who lives in the house, and he knows we're here?'

Jack felt his stomach do flip-flops. 'OK, you're right,' he whispered. 'Let's get out of here.'

'You go first, I'll follow,' said Ella.

'Why can't you go first?' said Jack.

'Because I don't think I remember the way through all the branches and stuff,' said Ella. 'Do we go left or right outside the shelter?'

Jack paused for a moment to think. They could definitely hear shouting now, as well as a strange rising and falling, whining noise. They could also hear fireworks somewhere, as it was Bonfire Night or New Year's Eve. It was now almost as dark as night, and there was a strange smell in the air, like burning rubber. Jack realised he couldn't see anything of the garden any more, as it was covered by some sort of mist or smoke.

'Jack, let's just *go*,' said Ella. 'I don't like it here, I want to go *now*!'

Then they heard the sound of a whistle being blown repeatedly, and a man's voice shouted loudly from the direction of the street.

'Take cover!' shouted the man.

Jack felt Ella grasp his hand. He took a deep breath and launched himself through the doorway, pulling Ella behind him and hoping that they would be able to find the way back to the hole in the fence.

He looked up and, above in the gloom, he saw the underside of an enormous aeroplane pass over, trailing a plume of fire behind it, accompanied by a deafening roar of engines. Before he could even blink, there was a blinding flash of light and he felt himself hurled backwards. Then everything went black.

Chapter Four
Escape from the Shelter

Jack felt for a moment as if he was lying in his own bed and had just woken up, but then he felt something underneath him move. He heard Ella say 'Ow, get off of me!'

He opened his eyes and realised he was back in the shelter and had fallen backwards on top of her. It took a few seconds for them to disentangle themselves.

'What…what happened?' said Ella, in a confused voice.

Without pausing for thought, Jack looked out of the doorway and saw that the smoke seemed to have cleared, and all had gone quiet.

'Quick,' he hissed at Ella. 'Now's our chance. Run!'

The two children dashed out of the shelter and pushed their way through the trees, following the trail of bent and broken branches they had made on their way in.

'Ow!' said Ella, as a branch whipped back and hit her arm.

'Keep moving!' said Jack.

It seemed as if they had been running for ages

before they saw the hole in the fence. They both squeezed through. Jack shoved the loose planks back in place and they both collapsed on the grass in Jack's garden.

'Has the man who was shouting at us gone?' asked Ella. 'And what about all that smoke and stuff? Is the house next door on fire?'

Jack at last managed to get his breath back. 'Let me look,' he said. He got up and peered cautiously through the gap in the fence. There didn't seem to be anyone around. The old house was still and silent.

He noticed the sky was still quite dark, and he looked up to see thick black clouds rolling past rapidly above him. In the distance there was a rumble of thunder and a flash of lightning. A big raindrop plopped down on his head, and within a few seconds, heavy rain was pouring down.

'It all looks OK,' said Jack, with a puzzled expression on his face. 'I don't think anyone saw us. We'd better get indoors quick, or we'll be soaked.'

'Don't say anything to your mom about this,' hissed Ella.

They rushed into the kitchen where they were met by Mrs Thomas.

'Goodness,' she exclaimed. 'You're soaked. I heard the thunder and thought you would have come in before the rain started.' She laughed. 'You both look like you've been dragged through a hedge backwards. What on earth have you been doing?

Jack was about to announce that they *had* been dragged through a hedge backwards, but then he felt Ella give him a sharp dig in the ribs. 'We were just playing,' he said.

'I thought you were supposed to be gardening,' said Mrs Thomas.

'Well we started to, but then we had to stop because of the rain,' said Ella, which was sort of true, so she didn't think she was telling a fib.

'Fair enough,' said Mrs Thomas, gazing out of the kitchen window. 'You can't do any more work now anyway. Look at that rain, it's coming down like stair rods.'

After briefly wondering what stair rods were, Jack decided he should cautiously find out if anything had happened next door.

'Mum,' he said. 'Did you hear any noises next door?'

Ella gave him a warning glance.

'What sort of noises?' asked Mrs Thomas.

'Erm, like a loud bang, and maybe some shouting?' said Jack, ignoring a second dig in the ribs from Ella, which was unseen by Jack's mother because she had her back turned while she prepared a snack for them.

'Yes,' said Mrs Thomas. 'Didn't you hear it? There was that huge clap of thunder and flash of lightning. It must have been quite close because I think it set off that car alarm in the street. I heard one of the neighbours shouting to someone to turn it off.'

'Oh,' said Jack. 'I guess that was what we heard too,' he said. He looked at Ella doubtfully.

The rain continued all afternoon, so while Mrs Thomas got on with her work, Jack and Ella sat in Ella's room on bean bags, talking about what had happened.

'That was so scary,' said Ella. 'I've never been in a lightning strike before.'

'Do you really think that's what happened?' said Jack.

'Of course,' said Ella. 'Think about it. That shack – or shelter, or whatever it is, has a metal roof. Metal attracts lightning in a storm. Didn't you know that?'

'I think so,' said Jack. 'Dad told me it's dangerous to go out on a golf course with an umbrella in a thunderstorm, as you might get struck by lightning.'

'Sure,' said Ella.

'But what about the man we heard shouting, and that weird noise, like a police car or a fire engine?' said Jack.

Ella thought for a moment. 'Your mom said she heard a car alarm in the street, and somebody shouting to someone else to turn it off. That must have been what we heard.'

'But I'm sure I heard the man say "take cover",' said Jack. 'Why would someone say that in a storm?'

'He was probably telling someone to get out of the rain,' said Ella.

'But it wasn't raining,' said Jack. 'It didn't start raining until we got back into our own garden. And what about the smoke, and those weird firework noises we heard. You must have heard them too?'

'I did, but it must have been thunder or something,' said Ella. 'The smoke was probably just someone burning trash, or leaves or something.'

'But we didn't see any smoke in our garden,' insisted Jack. 'Or in next door's garden when I looked back through the fence.'

37

Ella shrugged. 'I guess we just got a bit scared because we were in a creepy place. We should just forget it and move on. That's what my mom says to do if something you don't like happens.' She looked down and started to flick through the messages on her phone.

Jack bit his lip. 'What about that plane that flew over us, though?'

'What plane?' said Ella.

'It flew right over us when we came out of the shelter.'

'I didn't see any plane.'

'You must have done,' insisted Jack. 'It was so low I thought it was going to hit us, and it had fire coming out of it.'

Ella folded her arms. 'If you remember, you fell backwards on top of me when the lightning flashed. I couldn't see a thing because your head was in my face.'

'Sorry,' said Jack sheepishly. 'But I did see a plane.'

'OK, so what?' said Ella. 'Back home I see airplanes flying over New York all the time. It's probably the same here.'

'I know what a normal plane looks like,' said Jack. 'But this was different.'

'How?' said Ella. She put her phone down and looked up.

'It was really low, like it was landing, ' said Jack. 'And it was on fire.'

'Don't be stupid,' said Ella. 'If a plane was on fire over London, there would be something on the news about it. Check online, I bet you don't find anything.'

Jack got his tablet and they did an internet search for 'plane on fire over London.' Nothing came up, except some old photos and reports from a long time ago.

'See,' said Ella. 'You must have imagined it.'

'I didn't,' insisted Jack. 'I saw it. And I remember something else. It was old.'

'How can you tell if an airplane is old?' said Ella. 'They all look pretty much the same to me.'

'It was one of those ones that have, what do you call them...those things that go round.' Jack struggled to find the right word, and then remembered it. 'Propellers. It had two propellers. One on each wing. It was so close that I saw them spinning round.'

'I'm pretty sure you just imagined it,' said Ella. She went back to scrolling through her text messages.

Jack sighed. He had the horrible feeling of knowing he had definitely seen something, but also of knowing he didn't have any way to prove it. He looked down at his tablet and glanced at the old pictures that had come up during the search for news of a burning plane over London.

'That's it!' he shouted.

'That's what?' said Ella.

Jack pointed to a grainy black and white photo of an old-fashioned aeroplane on the screen.

'That's the plane I saw,' he said. 'I remember that big curved window at the front. Well, it was almost like that,' he added, as he clicked on the photo for more information. A website about the Second World War opened and they both saw the black and white photograph of the plane.

'It's called a…' Jack paused as he struggled to pronounce the name. 'A…Heinkel He 111'. He started to read out the paragraph below the photo.

'One of the most nu…'

'Numerous,' prompted Ella, who was reading over his shoulder.

'One of the most numerous German bombing planes of the Second World War,' continued Jack.

'You can't have seen that,' said Ella.

'Why not?' asked Jack.

'Look,' said Ella, pointing her finger at the screen. 'It says there are only five of them left in the whole world. There's only one in England, at the RAF Museum in Hendon.'

'Hey,' said Jack. 'That's quite near here. I remember seeing a poster about it on the tube.'

'That still can't have been the one you saw,' said Ella. 'Look, it says here, "no longer operational." That means it can't fly anymore.'

Jack frowned. 'Well…maybe they fixed it, and got it flying again.'

'But then there would definitely be something in the news about that, especially if it caught on fire like you said,' replied Ella. 'Look Jack, I know you think you saw something, but it was probably just your imagination. We were pretty scared by that thunderstorm. And when you get scared, your mind plays tricks on you. '

'I suppose so,' said Jack.

That evening, when Mr Thomas had come home from work and they had all finished supper, Ella went off to her room to talk to some of her friends on her phone, and Mrs Thomas went upstairs to finish off some of her work. Jack stayed in the sitting room next to his father, who was watching the TV news. Jack sat quietly, watching the screen carefully. He was hoping he might see a report that might make sense of what he had seen earlier that day.

'You're not normally interested in the news,' said Mr Thomas. 'I'm glad to see you're taking an interest in current affairs.'

The news came to an end, without any mention of burning planes over London. The weather reporter came on, talking about the big storm that had hit the city that afternoon. He then announced that tomorrow would be fine. Mr Thomas clicked off the set with the remote control.

'Good news about the weather,' he said. 'You'll be able to keep on working on the garden tomorrow.'

Jack took a deep breath. 'Dad…' he said.

'Yes?' said Mr Thomas.

'If a plane caught fire over London, would it be on the news?'

Mr Thomas thought for a moment. 'I should think so. That would be quite big news. It would have to make an emergency landing somewhere.'

'What's an emergency landing?'

'It's when a plane has to land right away, for example if it caught fire, like you say. There might not be time to get to the airport, and it would have to land somewhere like a big field, so that the passengers could get out.'

'And would that be on the news?' asked Jack.

'Oh definitely,' said Mr Thomas. 'It happened a few years ago in New York. Just about the time Ella was born, I think. The pilot had to land on the river. It was on the news for weeks and they even made a film about it. Why do you ask?'

Jack tried to sound uninterested. 'Oh, no reason,' he said. 'I was just imagining what would happen if a plane caught fire over London.'

Mr Thomas looked at Jack over the top of his glasses. 'Hmm,' he said. 'You've got quite an active imagination, haven't you? I think that comes from your mother. She's the creative one in the family.'

'I suppose,' said Jack.

'Right,' said Mr Thomas. He looked at his watch. 'It's past your bedtime young man. Off you go and do your teeth.'

Once he was tucked up in bed, Jack found that he couldn't sleep. He kept wondering whether he really had imagined seeing the plane. After all, he thought, it did seem as if he'd just woken up after he'd fallen back into the shelter. Had he dreamed it? He didn't think so. Dreams never seemed that real to him, but he could remember almost every detail of the plane.

Jack decided it was pointless trying to get to sleep, so he got out his tablet and switched it on. He wasn't supposed to look at it after lights out, but he decided that because what he wanted to look at was educational rather than a game or something like that, that it was OK.

He did an internet search on 'Heinkel bomber plane on fire over London'. A lot of results came up, all to do with the Second World War. He realised he would never be able to read through all the results. Then he had an idea. He did a new search, this time for 'Heinkel bomber plane on fire over Northgate, London.'

Jack's eyes widened as he saw the first result from the search engine. It showed a grainy black and white photograph of a plane very similar to the one he had seen from the shelter; behind it was a long trail of fire and black smoke which was coming from one of the propellers. The plane was passing very low over some houses. Jack clicked on the photograph and landed on some sort of local history website. Next to the photograph was a short paragraph:

A German Heinkel He111 bomber plane on fire, passing low over Cotswold Gardens, Northgate, NW12. A few moments after this photograph was taken, the aircraft crash-landed in a nearby park.

Jack felt his heart beat faster with excitement. So he hadn't imagined it! But why, he wondered, hadn't all this been on the news? He then noticed the final sentence of the paragraph.

Photograph taken by Northgate Gazette *reporter, 13 August 1940.*

They must mean 13 August 2020, thought Jack, as that was today's date. It must be a mistake. He blinked and looked again. But there was no doubt about it. It definitely said 1940. He looked again at the picture and saw that Cotswold Gardens was empty. Normally both sides were lined with parked cars, but in this photograph he could only see one car, an old-fashioned one with an open roof. He had never seen a car like that except in a museum.

Next to the car was a figure in black; Jack looked closer and saw it was what looked like some sort of army man, wearing one of those round metal helmets he'd seen in old films. In small white letters on the helmet, Jack could just make out the word POLICE. The man was pointing at the plane and had something in his mouth; it looked like he was blowing a whistle. Jack had never seen a policeman dressed like that either.

There was no way, he thought, that photograph could have been taken of something that happened today. Jack's thoughts started whirring around in his head very quickly. He took a deep breath and tried to make sense of it all. Had he somehow seen something from the shelter that had happened 80 years ago? What could it all possibly mean?

Jack wondered about speaking to Ella about it, but it was really late now and he was worried he would get into trouble if his parents caught him out of bed. Before long, he started to be unsure if he was awake or dreaming, and finally fell into a deep sleep.

Chapter Five
Back to the Shelter

The next day was bright and sunny. After breakfast, Mr Thomas went off to work as usual and Mrs Thomas went into her room to do her drawings, leaving Jack and Ella on their own in the garden.

Jack was digging over the vegetable patch at the bottom of the garden, while Ella cut back some of brambles and ivy which had crept over the fence from the old house next door. Once he was sure that his mother was inside the house and they could not be overheard, he turned to his cousin.

'Ella, I think there's definitely something weird going on with that shelter next door,' he said.

Ella stopped digging for a moment and sighed. 'Oh Jack, you don't still think you saw some old airplane? I'm sure it was just your imagination.'

'It wasn't, Ella, I'm sure of it,' said Jack, and told her about the old photograph he had seen online.

Ella bit her lip. 'Hmm,' she said. 'It does sound weird. But I don't see how you could see something that happened all that time ago.'

Jack thought for a moment. 'Do you believe in

ghosts?' he asked.

Ella laughed. 'Come on Jack. There's no such things as ghosts.'

'But lots of people say they've seen them,' said Jack. 'What if what I saw was sort of like a ghost, from the old days?'

'You mean like a ghost airplane?' asked Ella.

'Why not?' said Jack. 'I've heard of there being ghost ships in the old pirate days. You can even get beer called Ghost Ship. My dad drinks it sometimes. So why not a ghost plane?'

'It sounds kind of crazy,' said Ella.

Just then Jack looked up at the old house next door. Something was not right, but at first, he couldn't think what it was. Then he realised what it was.

'Ella, look at the house next door.'

'What about it?' said Ella, squinting up at the back of the building.

'The top window, look. The curtains have been opened.'

'How do you know?'

'I'm sure they were closed before,' said Jack. 'I remember because I couldn't see anything.'

'I thought you said you saw light from a flashlight in there?'

'No, that was the window on the other side.'

'Well, so what? Maybe whoever lives there just opened the curtains?'

'But nobody lives there,' said Jack. 'We never see or hear anyone and they don't have any lights on at night. So who opened the curtains? What if…?'

'What if what?' asked Ella suspiciously.

'What if there's a ghost in there?' said Jack. 'And it's got something to do with the old plane that I saw.'

Ella sighed. 'Jack, how old are you? We saw thunder and lightning, that's all, and you imagined the rest.'

Jack threw down his spade and sat down on the lawn in a sulk. Ella laughed, but when she realised how upset he was, she walked over to him and sat next to him.

'I didn't mean to laugh at you,' she said. 'But really, there's no point getting upset. Your mind played a trick on you, that's all.'

Jack continued to stare down at the grass without saying anything.

'OK, look,' said Ella. 'Why don't we go back through the fence? To make sure that there's nothing creepy or weird going on. You'll see that it's just an old shelter and that's all.'

Jack looked up. 'But what if…'

'There you go again,' said Ella. 'What if nothing. There's nobody in that house, I'm sure of it. If there was we would have seen or heard somebody by now. It's abandoned. Come on, this gardening is boring anyway. Let's check out the shelter again. I told my friend Cassie what we found and she doesn't believe me, so I need to send her a picture anyways.'

'OK,' said Jack, somewhat reluctantly.

Once they had checked that nobody was watching, Jack prised open the loose fence boards and they stepped through into the overgrown garden. The sky was much brighter than the day before, and the garden looked much less creepy in strong sunlight.

After a few moments of scrambling through the undergrowth, they pushed their way through the hedge to the small clearing and the shelter.

'Let's take a selfie,' said Ella. 'Cassie will be really jealous. She didn't believe me when I told her we sneaked into an old garden.'

The two children stood in front of the shelter and Ella snapped a picture, then after a few clicks sent it off to her friend in America.

'She'll be asleep right now because of the time difference,' said Ella, 'but when she wakes up she'll see it.'

'What do you mean, the time difference?' asked Jack.

'New York is five hours behind London,' said Ella. 'It's still the middle of the night there, so Cassie will be asleep.'

'I don't get it,' said Jack. He looked at his watch. 'How can it be nine o'clock here in London but the middle of the night in America?'

'It's kind of complicated to explain,' said Ella.

'You mean you don't know?' asked Jack.

Ella blushed slightly. 'No, I do, but it's just kind of confusing. It's something to do with how the world turns around. So when it's day in one place it can still be night someplace else.'

'Oh, OK,' said Jack, doubtfully. 'It doesn't really matter anyway. Let's go in the shelter again.'

They picked their way carefully down the concrete steps and stepped through the doorway into the shelter. The sun was much brighter today and shone through the doorway, lighting up the little room, and small beams of sunlight shone through the cracks in the metal ceiling. It all looked much less scary than yesterday, thought Jack.

'Hey look, there's more old junk here,' said Ella. She pointed to the pile of rusty old tin cans on the crate in the corner, where Jack had found the old gas mask. She took a picture with her phone and then started to rummage through some of the things.

'Look, there are some old magazines here,' she said, picking up a sheet of discoloured paper. She read out the title. '*Picture Post*. June 1940.' The magazine fell to pieces in her hand. 'Oh,' she said. 'That's a shame.'

'Here's some candles,' said Jack, pointing to a discoloured, dusty box on the floor. 'There's still some in here. That could be useful.'

Ella sat on the old bunk bed, taking care to sit only on the wooden edge instead of the old rusty wire frame, which looked a bit dangerous.

'Well,' she said, 'we've been here a while now and nothing weird or creepy has happened. Just like I said.'

'I suppose,' said Jack. He sat down next to Ella on the bunk. 'I suppose I *must* have imagined seeing that plane,' he added. 'Dad told me I have a very active imagination.'

'See,' said Ella. 'It's nothing to worry about. My friend Leah started imagining all kinds of things and getting scared about stuff all the time. Then she had to see a therapist. That's a kind of doctor, I think. But she's OK now. So it happens to lots of people.'

'I don't need to see a doctor,' said Jack. 'There's

nothing wrong with imagining…'

Jack didn't manage to finish his sentence because just then, there was an enormous crash, like thunder. They both felt the ground shake under them and noticed a ringing noise in their ears. Little bits of dust and soil fell down from the ceiling and they both coughed and spluttered. Then there was a distant rumbling, like thunder when it moves further away, and the sound of small explosions, like fireworks going off.

Jack noticed the rays of sun coming through the doorway had disappeared, and the light inside the shelter had dimmed. Once again he smelled smoke in the air.

'It's happening again, Ella!' he said. 'We've got to get out of here. Supposing we get struck by lightning?'

'Wait!' hissed Ella. 'It can't be another thunderstorm. The sky was totally clear when we came in. Just keep quiet, and wait. We've got to figure out what's going on.'

Once again they could hear sounds of shouting from the direction of the road.

'There's definitely somebody out there,' said Jack. 'We've got to hide, in case there really is someone in the house who's seen us. What if he's shooting at us?'

'OK,' said Ella. They both squeezed into the small space behind the storage crate in the corner, and tried to hide themselves as best they could.

The rumbling sound in the distance became a crashing sound, and they felt the ground tremble under their feet. There was a rattling noise on the metal roof of the shelter, and little bits of soil and dust started falling down from the ceiling on to their heads; they both coughed again and shook the debris out of their hair.

The sound of small explosions in the distance was constant now – *bang, bang, bang, bang,* like someone slamming an enormous car door over and over again.

Then they heard a sort of buzzing sound above them, like lots of motorbikes going very fast. They both looked up and saw, through the narrow opening, three aeroplanes passing over. Jack leapt to his feet, knocking over the crate as did so, and rushed to the doorway.

'They're the ones I saw!' he shouted. 'Look, Ella, the planes, I didn't imagine it!'

'I see them!' Ella called back, struggling to make herself heard over the noise of the planes as they passed over the shelter. It was so loud that it sounded as if they were next to a giant washing machine.

'I saw them Jack!' she shouted. 'Old planes, just like in the picture! But what….'

Before she could finish speaking, there was another enormous explosion, bigger than the last one, and both of them were thrown to the ground.

Several minutes must have passed before either of them dared move, or even speak. There were no more explosions or bangs, but they heard a strange wailing sound in the distance, that sounded like a long single note on a trumpet. After a few minutes even that stopped.

'Are you OK?' whispered Jack.

'I think so,' said Ella. 'How about you?'

'I'm alright,' said Jack. 'I don't think anyone's out there now.'

Ella sat up. 'Jack…' she began, then hesitated. 'What just happened?'

'I don't know,' said Jack. 'But I was right about the planes, wasn't I?'

'Yes…but…I don't like it here anymore. I don't know what's going on but there's something really scary about this place. Let's get out of here.'

They stood up and dusted themselves down. 'Urgh,' said Ella. 'I must be so dirty after lying on that dusty old floor.' She looked down at the floor, and her eyes widened.

'What's happened to the floor?' she said, pointing. 'What about it?' asked Jack.

'It was all gross and dirty before, with dead leaves and stuff, but look at it now. It's all clean. It looks like someone swept it.'

Jack shrugged and moved towards the doorway.

'Come on, let's get back to our garden before anybody sees us,' he said.

'Wait, Jack,' said Ella. 'Look at the roof.'

'Oh yeah,' said Jack. 'That big dent isn't there anymore.'

They both looked at the curved roof, which no longer sagged on one side.

'And the metal looks new,' said Ella. 'Like it's been cleaned too.'

'Someone's cleaned all the tin cans!' exclaimed Jack, pointing to the stack of junk in the corner which he had knocked over when the planes came past. He looked to his left and pointed to the bunk beds.

'And there's mattresses on those beds,' he said. 'How did they get there?'

'Jack,' said Ella, with fear in her voice, 'somebody hasn't cleaned the cans. Look, they're totally new. You can see the labels. The magazines are new, too.' She picked up the copy of *Picture Post* which had previously fallen to bits. It now looked as if it had just been bought from a shop.

'Did we fall asleep?' said Jack, cautiously. 'Could somebody have come in and cleaned up without us noticing?'

'No way,' said Ella. 'Let's get out of here, quick. Something weird's going on.'

Jack nodded and led the way out of the shelter. He was ready to dash through the undergrowth to the hole in the fence, but before he even reached the top of the concrete steps, he stopped so quickly that Ella bumped into him.

Jack blinked and rubbed his eyes. The garden had completely changed. The hedge was still in front of them, but it was much lower than before, and neatly trimmed. The gap in the hedge they had squeezed through before was now wide enough to pass through easily. Through it Jack could see the garden beyond.

All the trees and weeds had gone and there was just a lawn with some flowerbeds on each side. On his right Jack noticed a greenhouse, like the one they had smashed the day before, but this one was different somehow. It looked almost brand new. Next to it, propped up against the glass, was a red lawnmower, almost identical to the one they had found hidden in the weeds; but this looked very new also.

'Do you see what I see?' whispered Jack, who crept away from the gap in the hedge so that he could not be seen.

'Yes,' whispered Ella. 'We're in a different garden. And the houses are different too.'

Jack peeked through the gap in the hedge again and saw that Ella was right. The old, derelict house was now a new looking house, with freshly painted doors and windows. The windows had strange patterns on them, as if someone had criss-crossed them with white sticky tape. He glanced next door and saw that the house looked much the same, with similar patterns on the windows.

'Where are we?' said Ella. 'How did we get here? Does the shelter have some other door, or something?'

They both turned to look at the shelter. From outside it did not look much different, but the metal walls, which had previously looked old and rusty, were now new and shiny, and most of the front was covered with big brown bags stacked neatly like bricks in a wall.

'There's no other door,' said Jack, walking around the shelter.'

'Then where are we?' said Ella again.

Jack heard a familiar rattling noise and looked to his left; he saw the long railway bridge that he was now used to seeing from his bedroom window. A tube train crossed over it.

'I don't know what's going on,' he said, 'but I think we're in the same place. That's the tube line.' He turned to his right and pointed to the house next door. 'Look up there. 'That's my bedroom window.'

'It can't be,' said Ella. 'It looks different.'

'Only one way to find out,' said Jack. 'Let's get back through the fence.'

They peeked through the gap in the hedge to make sure nobody was in the garden, or watching from the house, and dashed across the lawn, past the greenhouse, to where Jack guessed the hole should be.

There was no hole to be found.
Jack pushed at all of the planks in the fence, trying to find one which would move, but nothing budged.

'I told you, this isn't the same garden,' said Ella.

'It must be,' said Jack. 'We must have fallen asleep for ages, and somebody must have come and cleared the garden and mended the fence.'

'And I guess they cleaned the shelter while we were in it, and painted the houses a different colour too?' asked Ella, sarcastically. 'Don't be stupid.'

'Well I don't know what else could have happened,' said Jack angrily. 'You thought there must be another door in the shelter, and that's *really* stupid.'

'Keep your voice down,' hissed Ella.

'OK,' said Jack, who was trying to keep calm. 'Let's just walk out the garden by the side of the house, and walk round to my house. Then we can get inside and my mum will be able to explain what's happened.'

Ella nodded, and they both crept around the edge

of the garden towards the little gate by the side of the house that led out into the street. This time Ella led the way, and this time, it was Ella's turn to freeze and for Jack to bump into her.

There was a boy standing in front of them.

For a few seconds nobody spoke. The boy was about eleven years old and had a mop of dark hair which flopped over his forehead. He was wearing a white shirt and a knitted sleeveless v-neck pullover. He also wore baggy grey shorts, brown shoes and long grey socks pulled up to his knees. He blinked at them through round glasses.

Ella was the first to speak. 'Hi…er…we were just leaving.'

The boy looked a little disappointed.

'Oh,' he said. 'Did you get caught in the raid?'

'The…raid?' asked Jack.

'Yes,' replied the boy. 'The air raid. I saw you coming out of the shelter. I suppose you must have run in from the street.'

'We're really sorry,' said Ella. 'We're going now anyway.'

'It's alright,' said the boy. 'Mother doesn't mind. Didn't you see the sign on the gate?'

'Er…no,' said Jack.

'It says "if you are caught in an air raid you may use the shelter in this garden."' Mother doesn't like us using it but she said it was a waste to leave it empty, so she put that sign up. Nobody's used it though, except the milkman once, but that turned out to be a false alarm anyway because no bombers came over.'

'Bombers?' said Jack.

'Yes, you know,' said the boy. 'German bomber planes. They're usually trying to hit the railway line. I say, are you quite alright?' He peered at them through his glasses. 'You look like you've had a shock. An air raid can do that to people. I'll tell mother to give you some Ovaltine.'

'German bomber planes?' whispered Jack. His mouth had gone dry and he felt as if his legs were about to give way. He took a deep breath and looked the boy in the eye.

'What year is this?' asked Jack.

'Gosh,' said the boy. 'You might have shell shock.'

'What the heck is that?' asked Ella.

'It's when people go barmy after a bombshell explodes near them,' the boy explained.

Jack thought quickly. 'Maybe,' he said. 'I think we might have shell shock just a tiny bit. We just can't seem to remember what day it is.'

'Oh, that's not too bad then,' said the boy. 'That's not a bad case of shell shock. Some chaps got it in the last war and went completely potty. You're probably just a bit dazed. Well to set the record straight, it's Wednesday the fourteenth of August, 1940.'

Jack and Ella looked at each other and their mouths fell open. They had somehow travelled 80 years into the past!

Chapter Six
The Boy from the Past

'I don't believe you,' shouted Ella to the boy. 'This is a trick. It's got to be. It's a joke, like one of those TV shows where they play tricks on people.'

The boy stared open-mouthed at Ella. Jack tried to speak to her.

'Ella, I don't think it's a trick…'

'It *is* a trick,' insisted Ella, 'and I'll prove it to you. Come on.'

She grabbed Jack by the arm and marched him through the small gate at the side of the house that led to the street. Before he had even had a chance to look around him, she had pulled him into the garden of the house next door – Jack's house.

Ella banged loudly on the front door. Jack noticed that the door was different; instead of the modern white one he was used to, it was an old brown wooden door with a little stained-glass panel.

Moments later an old woman with white hair, wearing a long black dress, opened the door.

'Yes?' she said, peering at the children.

'Where's Aunt Claire and Uncle James?' Ella demanded.

'Aunt Claire and Uncle James?' asked the woman. 'I think you must have the wrong house, young lady.' She turned to close the door.

'Wait,' said Ella. She pushed her foot into the doorway before the woman could close the door. 'How long have you lived here?' she asked.

'I don't see that it's any concern of yours,' said the woman, 'but I have been living here for six years – since 1934.'

'But that's impossible,' said Ella. 'What about Aunt Claire and Uncle James – I mean, Mr and Mrs Thomas?'

'I'm sorry,' said the woman, 'there is nobody of that name here. You've obviously got the wrong house.'

'I don't believe you!' said Ella angrily. 'Let me inside, I want to find my aunt and uncle!' She tried to get past the woman into the hallway.

'How dare you!' said the woman. 'Get out this instant, or I shall inform the police!'

Ella stepped back quickly as the door was slammed shut. She leaned forward to bang on the door again, but her arm was gently pulled down by Jack.

'Look,' said Jack. 'There's no way this could be a trick.'

Ella turned round to see that Jack was pointing to the road. She looked along Cotswold Gardens, and saw that every house had changed. They all had old-fashioned wooden doors, and every window had those strange criss-crossings of tape on the glass.

'What's that tape on the windows for?' said Ella.

The boy, who had been watching them from the garden gate, stepped forward.

'Don't you have that at your house?' he asked. 'That's sticky tape to stop the windows breaking if a bomb goes off nearby. You can see it works because that bomb up the road didn't break any of these windows.'

'Bomb...?' said Ella. She looked to the end of the road and realised where the smoke in the air was coming from. One of the houses had lost its roof; bricks and broken bits of wood lay in the road and flames were licking at its broken windows. A fire engine was next to the house and firemen were spraying water from a hose onto the wreckage.

'Let's go and look,' said the boy. 'We might find some shrapnel.'

'What's shrapnel?' asked Jack.

'Don't you know *anything*?' said the boy. 'Shrapnel's bits of bombs and bullets and things that you find lying in the road after an air raid. Sometimes it's still warm. Come on.'

The three children began to walk towards the house but before long, a man approached them. Jack recognised him from the old photograph online – he was wearing one of those round helmets with 'POLICE' painted on it in white letters.

The policeman waved them away. 'Clear off, you lot,' he said angrily. 'We've just heard there might be more planes coming over. Go home and stay there. I don't want to see you out in this road again.'

Ella started to speak but the boy took her by the arm.

'Come on,' he said. 'Best to do what he says. We'd better get back to my garden.'

The children went back to the garden and sat down behind the little hedge, next to the shelter. Jack and Ella were silent.

'Look here,' said the boy. 'We'd better introduce ourselves. My name's Peter. Peter Bennett. What's yours?'

'I'm Jack,' said Jack. 'Jack Thomas. This is my cousin Ella.'

Ella didn't say anything. She just sat staring at the ground as the boys talked.

'Is she alright?' whispered Peter to Jack.

'We've both had a bit of a shock,' said Jack. 'You see we're…well we're sort of lost. I mean, we don't know how we got here.'

'Is that why you thought next door was your house, Ella?' said Peter.

Ella did not reply.

'Sort of,' said Jack. 'I don't know how to explain it. We're not really from around here.'

'I thought so,' said Peter. 'I've never seen you before, but that's because nearly all the children around here left in the evacuation.'

'What does evacuation mean?' asked Jack.

'There you go again,' said Peter. 'I guessed you weren't from around here because you don't seem to know very much about what's going on. The evacuation was last year, when the war started. Most children had to go and live in the country for safety. I went too, but mother said she was lonely so they sent me back here for the school hols as there hadn't been any bombs. Now there have been some and they say it's going to get worse, so I might have to go away again soon. I don't have any friends around here anyway, so it's a bit dull.'

'Oh yeah!' said Jack. 'I remember now. We learned about evacuation in a school project. Every child had to move away, and they all had to have a label with their name and address on it.'

Peter smiled. 'That's right. I say, perhaps you're getting over the shock now and your memory's coming back?'

Jack wriggled on the ground. He had absolutely no idea what to say. 'Sort of,' he said.

'And I also guessed you're not from here because of your clothes,' said Peter. I've never seen a girl wearing those funny sort of stockings before, like Ella has. They're awfully jolly.' He pointed to her sparkly purple leggings.

'Thanks,' said Ella. 'And I like your glasses too. They're kind of retro.'

'Thanks – I think,' said Peter. 'And I've never seen a boy your age wearing longs, either.'

'Longs?' asked Jack.

'Yes, you know,' said Peter, pointing to Jack's jeans. 'Long trousers. Every boy I know wears shorts, until he's fourteen. Where are you from, exactly?'

'It's a bit difficult to explain where we're from,' said Jack. 'It could take a while.'

'You've made me curious now,' said Peter. 'Let's have a drink first though,' said Peter. 'I'm dying of thirst. You wait here and I'll fetch some lemonade.'

Before Jack could answer, Peter had dashed up the

garden and gone into the house.

'Ella,' hissed Jack. 'What shall we say to him? I think we should tell him about the shelter, and about travelling to the past. He might be able to help us.'

'I don't believe any of this,' said Ella, in a sulky voice. 'I still think it's some kind of trick. I don't know who's behind it but I'm going to call my mom and get her to figure this out.'

Ella took her phone out of the pocket of her hoodie and scrolled through her contacts until she found her mother's number, then held the phone to her ear. Jack watched as after a few seconds, she frowned and dialled again.

'It's not working,' said Ella who was now scrolling through more of her contacts and dialling them. 'All the numbers are unavailable. There must be something wrong with the signal.' She stood up and walked across the garden, holding her phone up in the air.

'Did you get a signal in our garden, before we went in the shelter?' asked Jack.

'Sure, you know I did, I was always texting,' said Ella.

'Ella,' said Jack. 'I think you're right that there's no signal….'

'Told you,' said Ella, cutting him off before he could finish. 'Maybe your wi-fi's in range,' she added. 'I'll try that.'

She fiddled with the phone for a minute and then frowned. 'There's no signal, anywhere. None of the houses around here seem to have wi-fi.'

'I was going to say, Ella,' said Jack, 'I think there's

no signal because they didn't have mobile phones in 1940. They didn't have wi-fi either.'

'But…it can't be 1940, it just can't,' said Ella. She punched her fist onto the grass.

'I can't see any other explanation,' said Jack. 'Somehow, we've travelled through time.'

Ella sighed. 'Then that means there's no point trying to call my mom anyway. She hasn't even been born yet. Even my grandma wasn't born until 1950.'

'Well,' said Jack, 'I was going to say that as well, but I didn't want to upset you.'

'That's OK,' said Ella. 'I didn't mean to get mad at you. I guess it's just such a shock. We just have to figure out what we're going to do.'

Before they could discuss anything further, Peter emerged from the house with a jug of lemonade and some glasses on a tray. He poured a drink for each of them and they took long swigs from their glasses.

'This is really nice,' said Ella. 'What is it? I've never tasted lemonade like this before.'

Peter laughed. 'That's because there's no lemons in it,' he said.

'How can it be lemonade without lemons?' asked Jack.

'Mother makes it from a herb called lemon balm that she grows in the front garden,' he said. 'When was the last time you saw a real lemon in the shops?' he asked.

'Last week,' said Jack, and then clamped his mouth shut.

'Well you're lucky,' said Peter. 'Most shops can't get them at all now because of rationing.'

'What's rationing?' asked Ella.

'I knew it!' said Peter, jumping to his feet. 'I knew there was something funny about you two, and now I know what it is. '

'You do?' asked Ella, warily.

'Yes,' said Peter, with a broad grin. 'You're Americans! I could tell by your accents. Well, Ella's anyway. America isn't in the war, at least not yet, so I suppose they don't have rationing. I expect that's why you've never heard of it. It means not having enough food in the shops because of the war. We can't get some things, like lemons, and bananas. Does everyone in America wear clothes like you? Have you just arrived from there?'

'Erm…do you mind if I talk with my cousin alone for a moment?' asked Ella. Before Peter could reply she pulled Jack over to a corner of the garden.

'Listen, Jack. Don't say anything to him about coming from the future.'

'Why not?' asked Jack.

'Because he won't believe us, and he'll probably think we're crazy and if he tells his mom we might get locked up in, in, a nut house or something.'

'What's a nut house?'

'A place where they put crazy people.'

Ella pulled Jack back towards Peter and they sat down again. Ella composed herself and smiled at Peter.

'Yes, you're right, Peter. I am from America. I've only been here a few days. And yes, this is what girls wear in the states.' She pointed to her pink hoodie and purple leggings.

'Gosh,' said Peter. 'I've never met an American, but I love seeing American films at the pictures. Do you like *Buck Rogers*?' he asked.

'Who?' said Ella.

'It's a serial about a man who travels through time into the 25th century, it's awfully good. He…'

Before he could continue, Peter's voice was drowned out by a loud rising and falling siren which seemed to come from everywhere at once. It was similar to the long trumpet note they had heard earlier.

'Oh golly,' said Peter. 'Not again.'

'What's that noise?' asked Ella.

'That's the air raid siren – you *must* know what that is, even if you've only just arrived here. It goes off every time there's a raid coming. But we only had the all clear about half an hour ago.'

'What's the all clear?' asked Jack.

'That's the one that sounds when the bomber planes have gone,' explained Peter. 'But there must be another lot coming over.'

'What do we do?' said Ella. 'I don't like this, it's creeping me out.'

'"Keep calm and carry on",' said Peter, 'like the government posters say. You'll be alright in the Anderson,' he added, standing up.

He saw Jack and Ella looking at him blankly and sighed. 'It's where you were when the last raid came over. The Anderson shelter. Named after the chap who invented it, or something.'

A loud banging noise, like fireworks shot off in quick succession started up in the distance.

'Quick, you'd better hurry,' said Peter. 'That's the anti-aircraft guns, so the planes will be coming over any minute.'

Peter ushered Jack and Ella towards the shelter and bundled them inside, then turned to look behind him up at the sky. They could hear the strange buzzing, droning sound they had heard earlier.

'Can't see the planes yet, but that's them coming alright,' said Peter. 'Sounds like a lot of them. Get inside and lie low.'

'Aren't you coming in?' said Ella.

'No, I'd better get back to the house,' said Peter. 'Mother will be getting worried.'

'But what if your house gets hit by a bomb?' asked Jack.

'Don't worry,' said Peter. 'We never use this shelter any more. Mother calls it the tin coffin. Says she'd rather be in the house so we've got a Morrison shelter inside. It's like a sort of giant rabbit's cage. We'll be alright. See you after the raid!'

Peter began to jog across the lawn towards the house. The buzzing, droning sound was so loud now that Jack and Ella felt their teeth chattering. As they watched from the doorway of the shelter, they saw the sky darken as a row of black aeroplanes came into view above the house.

'Peter, look out!' shouted Ella. Peter looked up and then began to sprint across the lawn. There was a deafening whistling noise and then a blinding flash of light; Jack and Ella were pushed back into the shelter by a blast of hot air; and then once again, everything went black.

Chapter Seven
Uncle Geoff's Spaghetti

Jack felt again the strange sensation of waking up in his own bed, only to realise that, once again, he was lying on the floor of the shelter. This time, however, he was not on top of Ella, but rather, Ella was next to him.

'Jack, Jack, wake up,' she said, while shaking his shoulder.

Jack sat up. 'What happened?' he asked, rubbing his eyes.

'I think a bomb went off,' said Ella. 'It must have been those planes. But look, I think we've travelled through time again.'

Jack looked around the inside of the shelter and realised that the shiny new metal had now returned to a dirty, rusty colour, and the side of the roof was now caved-in and sagging as when they had first found it. The mattresses on the bunk beds had gone, and the bed frames were now covered with cobwebs and rust.

Ella peeked out of the doorway cautiously, ready to jump back in quickly if necessary. Instead, she turned to Jack with a big grin.

'Look, Jack,' she said. 'The garden. It's grown back again.'

Jack looked out as well, and sure enough, the neat garden of 1940 had returned to the overgrown, shadowy jungle they had left in 2020. The house now looked old again, and nothing like the one that they had last seen when Peter was running towards it as the planes came over.

'We're safe!' said Jack. 'We're back! Quick, let's get out of here before anything else happens.'

The two children scrambled up the shelter steps and raced through the undergrowth to the hole in the fence, which to their relief, was still there.

Once inside their own garden, they raced into the house, which looked just as they remembered it. Jack collided with Mrs Thomas, who had just come down to the kitchen to make a cup of tea.

'Aunt Claire,' said Ella. 'I'm so glad to see you!'

Mrs Thomas laughed. 'You've only just seen me at breakfast. What are you doing back in so soon?' she said. 'You've barely started on the garden.'

'Barely started?' said Jack. 'But we've been away for hours.' He then looked at his watch, and just to make sure, he looked at the clock on the kitchen wall. They had only been gone about five minutes.

'Hours?' said Mrs Thomas with a chuckle. 'Don't give me that. You've only been working on that flowerbed for about five minutes, so don't say you're tired already.'

'Erm, we just came in for a glass of water, Aunt Claire', said Ella. 'It's thirsty work in that garden,' she added.

Mrs Thomas gave them each a glass of water and then peered at them. 'Are you two alright?' she asked. 'You look awfully tired, like you've just run a mile.'

'We're just working hard, mum!' said Jack.

'Well get back to it then,' said Mrs Thomas. 'Your Uncle Geoff's coming round for supper tonight, and I want to start putting some stuff in the slow-cooker.'

The two children then dashed back into the garden. Once they were out of sight, they flopped down on the lawn.

Ella took out her phone and squinted at the screen in the sunlight. 'And I've got a signal,' she said happily. 'I'm going to call my mom. Oh, wait, it's still really early back in New York. I guess I'd better wait.'

'I can't believe it,' said Jack. 'We actually travelled through time. Hey, don't you think we should tell my mum about it?'

Ella paused for a moment, frowning. 'I don't think. She would probably just think we were making it up.'

'But it's the most amazing thing I've ever heard of,' said Jack.

'I know,' replied Ella. 'But...how could we prove it? And also it would mean she would find out we'd been sneaking next door and breaking stuff in the garden. We might get into a lot of trouble.'

'Oh yeah,' said Jack. 'I suppose so. Best keep it quiet I suppose. And we'd better start doing some more digging or mum will wonder what we've been doing.'

The two children began digging over the

flowerbeds, and both gradually began to calm down following their strange experience in the shelter. After a while, Ella stopped digging.

'Jack,' she said. 'What do you think happened to Peter? Do you think he got hit by a bomb?'

Jack thought for a moment. 'I didn't think about that. He was running pretty fast into the house though, so I think he was alright.'

'But…' said Ella, 'we can't be sure. What if he got hurt?'

A thought struck Jack. 'If he got blown up then wouldn't the house be blown up as well, and so the house next door wouldn't be there now, would it?'

'But what if they just mended the house?' said Ella. 'Peter could have got hurt, or maybe even killed.'

Jack started giggling. He tried not to, but found he couldn't stop.

'What's so funny?' said Ella angrily.

'Why do you keep asking about Peter?' he said. 'I know why. I think you fancy him.'

'*What*?' said Ella angrily. 'What the heck does that mean?'

'Like, you really like him,' said Jack, still giggling. 'Ooh, Peter,' he continued, trying to make his voice sound like Ella's. 'I love your glasses, they're *sooo* retro.'

Ella's jaw dropped open. 'Jack Thomas, shut *up*,' she said, and punched him on the shoulder.

'What if we go back again?' said Ella.

'What?' said Jack. 'Are you serious? After we nearly got blown up by a bomb?'

'I *am* serious,' said Ella. 'Jack, we went back in time.

Nobody's ever done that before, at least, not anyone I've ever heard of. It would be awesome if we could do it again. Just think of all the stuff we could find out, and the things we could see.'

'And the people we could see,' said Jack. 'Like Peter!' He then started giggling again until Ella raised her fist and threatened to punch him.

'Alright stop,' said Jack, laughing. 'Maybe we could try to go back. But we need to find out a bit more about what's going on first. We don't know anything about it. Why's the shelter taking us back in time? And how do we know we won't get stuck in the past if we go back?'

'Hmm,' said Ella. 'I guess you've got a point. But how can we find out anything about time travel? It's not like we can just go to your mom and dad and say, like 'Hey, Aunt Claire and Uncle James, we've found a secret time machine and we just want some advice on how it works before we use it again.'

'I suppose you're right,' said Jack. Then a thought struck him. 'Hey, wait. I just remembered – mum said that Uncle Geoff was coming to supper tonight.'

'So?' said Ella. 'I don't think I know him, he must be on your dad's side of the family.'

'He is,' said Jack. 'He's my dad's older brother. He's a sort of…well a sort of mad professor.'

Ella's eyes widened. 'Do you think he knows about stuff like time travel?'

Jack nodded. 'Probably. If anyone does, Uncle Geoff does. He's always talking about things like that. Space, and planets, and black holes and stuff. Don't tell anyone but my dad says he's a bit weird.'

'What's weird about him?' asked Ella.

'Well,' said Jack. 'He's got weird hair and clothes, and he's always nodding and saying "yes, yes, yes" before he says anything.'

Ella laughed. 'He sounds funny.'

'You'll see,' said Jack. 'Bet you the first thing he says to you when he meets you tonight is "yes, yes yes."'

Ella and Jack both laughed. 'OK,' said Ella. 'Let's try and find out from him as much as we can about time travel. But don't tell him anything about the shelter, or he might get suspicious.'

Later that day after they had finished working in the garden, Jack and Ella heard a strange rattling, roaring noise in front of the house. They looked out to see a rusty old car, trailing clouds of smoke behind it, pulling into the drive. After a loud bang and a rattle the engine stopped. A tall, gangly man stepped out.

'Uncle Geoff!' shouted Jack and rushed over to meet him. Uncle Geoff stuck out his hand.

'Yes, yes, yes, it's young Jack, isn't it? Shake my hand.'

They shook hands as Ella watched. She couldn't help smiling because Jack had correctly predicted that Uncle Geoff's first words would be "yes, yes, yes."' She also thought he was one of the funniest looking men she'd seen. He had wild curly hair which stuck out from his head and wore thick glasses on the end of his nose.

Although he was wearing a dark suit, like Mr Thomas wore to go to work, he wasn't wearing a white shirt and tie with it; instead, he wore one of those colourful shirts covered in pictures of palm trees and flowers, like people wear on the beach. His trousers were held up by a brightly coloured belt with a rainbow pattern. Instead of formal black shoes, he wore brown sandals which revealed bare feet and hairy toes.

'This is my cousin, Ella,' said Jack.

'Yes, yes, yes,' said Uncle Geoff.

Jack and Ella burst out laughing but Uncle Geoff didn't notice. He just carried on talking. 'You're on the other side of the family of course. Don't think I've seen you since you were a baby. Yes, yes, yes.'

Jack and Ella started laughing again. By this time Mr and Mrs Thomas had come out into the front garden to greet Uncle Geoff, and Mrs Thomas suggested they all go inside as supper was ready.

They had spaghetti bolognaise, which was Jack's favourite. After they had nearly finished eating, Jack took a deep breath and decided the time was right to ask Uncle Geoff about time travel.

'Uncle Geoff,' he said cautiously.

'Yes, yes yes?' asked Uncle Geoff, whose mouth was full of spaghetti.

Jack looked at Ella and almost started to get the giggles, but managed to keep it under control.

'Uncle Geoff, is there such a thing as time travel? Only Dad says there aren't such things as Dr Who and travelling through time in real life.'

'Of course there aren't,' said Mr Thomas. 'They're just stories. Don't be silly Jack.'

'Yes, yes, no, no,' said Uncle Geoff, making a

waving motion to Mr Thomas. 'No, it's a good question Jack. Part of my research has been in just such an area.'

Mr Thomas rolled his eyes. 'You ought to get a proper job Geoff, not play around in laboratories all your life.'

'I'd rather be doing that than sitting around in a bank counting pennies all day,' said Uncle Geoff.

'No arguing please, boys,' said Mrs Thomas. 'Jack's asked a perfectly good question. I'm glad he's taking an interest in science. Go on, Geoff. What were you going to say?'

Mr Thomas snorted, and took a sip of his wine without replying.

'Yes, yes, yes,' said Uncle Geoff. 'Where was I? Ah yes. Time travel! Well, it might be possible in theory.'

'What do you mean "in theory"?' asked Ella.

'In science there are laws, and there are theories,' said Uncle Geoff. 'Laws are things we know are true, because we can see them happening.'

'Like the law of gravity?' asked Jack.

'What goes up, must come down,' said Ella.

'Exactly,' said Uncle Geoff, taking a big swig from the can of Coke next to him. 'So if I pick up this empty can and let it go, it will drop to the floor. That's the law of gravity. We know that happens because we can see it. Look.'

He picked up the can and dropped it on the floor, where it landed with a plop, and a big splash of Coke fizzed out onto the wooden floor.

'Oops, sorry,' said Uncle Geoff. 'Thought it was empty.'

'Never mind,' said Mrs Thomas with a laugh. 'I'll clean it up later.'

'Anyway,' said Uncle Geoff, 'that's a law. Now a theory is an idea about something, but we can't really see it so we can't prove it, but we think it *might* be possible.'

'Like the Theory of Relativity?' said Mrs Thomas.

'Yes, yes, yes,' said Uncle Geoff. 'Very good, Claire. Just what I was going to say. A scientist called Einstein came up with the Theory of Relativity.'

'How long will all this take, Geoff?' said Mr Thomas. 'It'll be the kids' bedtime soon.'

'I'll keep it simple,' said Uncle Geoff. 'Now this Einstein chap said that space and time might be sort of interwoven. Jumbled together, as it were. That could mean that time travel is possible.'

Jack felt his heart beating with excitement. 'How?' he asked.

'Hmmm,' said Uncle Geoff, and looked down at his plate for a moment. 'Yes, yes, yes, I know. Take this spaghetti, for example.' He pointed to several strands of spaghetti and little lumps of sauce that were left on his plate.

'What on earth are you talking about?' asked Mr Thomas.

'I may appear mad…' said Uncle Geoff.

'You *are* mad,' interrupted Mr Thomas with a chuckle.

'As I was saying, Jack,' continued Uncle Geoff. 'Imagine this strand of spaghetti on the plate is our universe and our time. Everything moves along this line. Here's where we are now, in 2020.' Jack and Ella craned their necks to see, as he placed a little blob of sauce on the spaghetti with his fork.

'But,' he continued, pushing another strand of spaghetti alongside, 'there could be another universe just like our own, sort of running alongside. But in that universe, the time is different, you see. In that universe, they might be further behind us in time. It might be a different year there. Name a year,' said Uncle Geoff to Jack and Ella.

'1940!' they said together, then looked at each other. Had they given away too much information? Jack wondered. Uncle Geoff carried on talking.

'1940! Excellent choice. Second World War. Battle of Britain. Bombs dropping all over the place! Whoosh, plop!' Uncle Geoff put a dollop of sauce on the other line of spaghetti. 'Now, see that blob of sauce – that's 1940 in another universe. It's there, but it's further back than we are.'

'But how can we travel through time?' asked Jack.

Uncle Geoff thought for a moment. 'It's just possible that we might be able to cross over into the universe in which it is still 1940. If, for example, our universe is close to that one at some point.' He used his fork to push the two strands of spaghetti closer together so that the two blobs of sauce were touching. 'See. Now, all we need to do is weave the strands together somehow, and we're in 1940.'

'But how on earth could that happen?' asked Mrs Thomas.

'It would take a colossal amount of energy,' said Uncle Geoff.

A thought struck Jack. 'Like a bomb, you mean?'

'Possibly,' said Uncle Geoff. 'But it would either have to be a very big bomb – bigger than anything ever made – or it would have to be at one very particular point in space, where our universe is very, very close to another universe.'

He picked up the big wooden pepper grinder from the table. 'Then, CRASH!' Uncle Geoff bashed the grinder down on to the two pieces of spaghetti. He lifted it up and showed the plate to Jack and Ella. 'See, the bits are merged. We've crossed into 1940!'

'You've made a mess again,' said Mrs Thomas. She took the grinder from Uncle Geoff, who looked at her sheepishly.

'Sorry,' he said. 'But that was the best way I could explain the theory.'

Jack started to ask another question. 'But what if…'

'That's enough questions, I think,' said Mr Thomas. 'Come on you two, it's late. You've had enough laws and theories for one day. It's bedtime now, and that's *my* law.'

Uncle Geoff laughed and then burped rather loudly.

'What goes down, must come up!' he said.

Jack and Ella burst out laughing and were then bundled upstairs by Mrs Thomas.

Just after lights-out, Jack thought he heard something through his open bedroom window. He peeked out from the side of the curtain, so that nobody could see him, and looked across to the old house next door. He blinked. He was sure he had just seen a torch flashing in the upstairs window again. He waited for a few moments, but nothing more happened. He shut the window tightly, despite the warmth of the evening, got into bed and pulled the covers up over his head before falling asleep.

Chapter Eight
Peter Becomes Suspicious

The next day Jack and Ella talked in the garden while, as usual, they worked on digging over the flowerbeds. It was early Saturday morning and Mr and Mrs Thomas were still in bed.

'I think we've got to check out the shelter again,' said Ella. 'Now's our chance while your mom and dad are sleeping.'

'I think we should tell them about it,' said Jack.

'Don't be stupid, Jack,' said Ella. 'They won't believe us.'

'Uncle Geoff might believe us, though,' said Jack. 'We could phone him.'

'I don't know,' said Ella. 'He seems a bit crazy to me. I think even if he believed us, your mom and dad wouldn't.'

'Alright,' said Jack. 'What if we went back in time again – but this time, we could prove we'd really done it?'

'Yes!' said Ella. 'That's more like it. I can shoot some video on my phone, and we can bring some stuff back to show we'd really been to 1940. Then they'd have to believe us'.

'What sort of stuff?' asked Jack.

'You know, newspapers and stuff like that,' said Ella. 'Then Uncle Geoff could take over and find out about how it works. You know, how the two bits of spaghetti are connected.'

Jack laughed. 'Yeah, what was all that about?' he asked. 'I didn't really get it.'

'Me neither,' said Ella. 'I think it means there's more than one universe. We just have to cross over into the universe where it's 1940.'

'Alright,' said Jack. 'Let's do it. But we need to be careful. I'm pretty sure I saw a torch flashing in the creepy old house again last night.'

'Oh Jack,' said Ella. 'You're such a baby sometimes. We're talking about going back in time, and you're worried about some crazy old guy with a torch who's probably completely harmless.'

A few moments later they climbed through the hole in the fence and scrambled into the old shelter. After about half an hour of waiting excitedly in the gloom for the sky to darken and the explosions to begin, they began to become bored. After an hour, they decided to give up.

'I don't get it,' said Ella. 'Nothing's happening.'

'Maybe it doesn't always work,' said Jack.

'But it's worked both times before,' said Ella. 'Let's wait just a bit longer.'

'There's another thing I'm worried about,' said Jack.

'What now?' sighed Ella. 'You're not still scared there might some weird guy living in the house over here? Wouldn't he have found us by now?'

'It's not that,' said Jack. 'It's…what if we go back to 1940 but then can't get back to our time? What if we get stuck there?'

Before Ella could reply, they heard a woman's voice calling outside the shelter.

Jack inhaled sharply. 'It's my mum! She must be wondering where we are. Quick, let's get back to the garden.'

The two children raced out of the shelter to the hole in the fence. Jack checked quickly that nobody was watching from the house, and they both climbed through and started working on the digging. A moment later, Mrs Thomas appeared from the kitchen.

'You are here, then,' she said. 'I called from the house to tell you that breakfast is ready but nobody answered.'

'Oh sorry, Aunt Claire,' said Ella. 'Jack and I were just, erm, just talking about history. We didn't hear you.'

Mrs Thomas gave them a funny look. 'Hmm, well, come on. You must be hungry after all that work.' She looked doubtfully at the flower beds, which had not been dug over much at all since she had last seen them.

After they had finished breakfast, Jack and Ella got up to go out into the garden again, but Mrs Thomas stopped them.

'Not you, Jack. I want you to tidy your room first. Ella keeps hers nice and neat, but yours looks like a bomb's gone off in it.'

'Aw, mum...' protested Jack, but before he could

finish, Ella grabbed him by the shoulder and marched him to the stairs.

'Good idea, Aunt Claire,' said Ella. 'In fact I'll go with Jack to make sure he cleans up.'

'Oh...er...that's helpful of you Ella,' said Mrs Thomas, looking rather puzzled. 'Off you go then.'

Once they were in Jack's room Ella closed the door.

'Jack, I've got it,' said Ella.

'Got what?' asked Jack.

'I think I know why the shelter didn't travel through time,' she said. 'It was what your mom said about your room that made me think. She said it looks like a bomb hit it.'

Jack laughed. 'Wonder what she'd think if we told her we'd seen a house that really had been hit by a bomb.'

'That's what I mean,' said Ella. 'Remember what Uncle Geoff said last night?'

'Something about two bits of spaghetti joining together.'

'No, not that. Well, yes, kind of. I mean, he said that there could be two universes, right? This one, and the one where it's still 1940.'

'Yes, I think so.'

'But he said it would take a huge amount of energy to cross between the two. What if that energy came from a bomb exploding nearby?'

'Hmm, I suppose it could,' said Jack. Then he grinned. 'Hey, I think I see what you mean. If a bomb goes off near the shelter, it travels through time.'

'Exactly,' said Ella. 'Remember each time we went

back in the shelter to 1940, there were bombs going off nearby.'

Jack thought for a moment. 'But wait. Uncle Geoff said it would need a really big explosion to blow us into another universe. He said a bigger bomb than has ever been made.'

'True,' said Ella. 'But he also said it could work if the two bits of spaghetti, I mean, the two universes were very close together. Maybe they just happen to be very close together right where that shelter is next door.'

'Maybe,' said Jack.

'So all we need to do is wait in the shelter. Eventually there will be another bomb explosion in 1940 and we'll go back.'

Jack frowned. 'But we can't just keep going back and sitting in there for ages. Mum might find out. She nearly got suspicious today.'

'I guess you're right,' said Ella with a sigh. 'Maybe we just try it a couple of times every day until we get lucky.'

'Wait!' said Jack. 'I've got an idea. We don't need to get lucky.'

'How do you mean?' asked Ella.

'Remember that website I told you about? The one that showed the picture of the old aeroplane?'

'I think so.'

'Let me get my tablet,' said Jack. He rummaged about among the pile of discarded books and clothes that littered the floor of his bedroom. 'Here it is.'

Jack eventually found the website, which was called 'Northgate Local History.' He scrolled to the section marked 'Northgate at war' and tapped it.

'Here it is. I remember I saw it before. It's a list of all the big bombing raids that happened around here in 1940.'

Ella's eyes widened. 'Hey, cool!' She looked at the text on the tablet screen. 'You're right, it even shows the time of some of them!'

'And the dates back in 1940 seem to be the same as ours,' said Jack. 'So when it was 13 August here, we went back to 13 August 1940.'

'That's right,' said Ella. 'And the second time it was 14 August, same as it was here. I remember Peter telling us.'

'So,' said Jack, 'maybe if we sit in the shelter on the same day as one of the air raids in 1940, we could get transported there.'

'Yes!' replied Ella enthusiastically. 'And there's something else. If we check the dates of all the bombing raids, we can be sure that we are in the shelter on one of those days, to get us back again to our own time.'

'Good idea,' said Jack. 'Glad I thought of it.'

Ella laughed. 'I think we both did, actually. Anyway, let's look at the dates.'

'Here they are,' said Jack, tracing his finger down the tablet screen. 'Air raids on Northgate. 1940. 13 August. 14 August. Then there was nothing until 17 August.'

Ella looked at a calendar on her phone. 'That's next Monday. Let's do it then. But we have to make sure we know when the next attack was, so that we can get back.'

'OK,' said Jack. 'Oh. It says that was on 19 August. But then there weren't any more.' Jack read out the text from the web page. '"...that was the last major bombing raid on Northgate for the remainder of the war. In September the German Air Force changed its plans and instead concentrated on bombing London's East End." That's miles from here. So we've got to make sure we're in the shelter on 19 August to get back home.'

'That's cool,' said Ella. 'That still gives us two days in 1940. What are you looking so worried about?'

'We can't just disappear for two days,' said Jack. 'Mum and Dad would go crazy. Remember today Mum even started to get a bit suspicious when we didn't reply after she called, and we'd only been gone an hour.'

'Hmm,' said Ella, frowning. 'I've been thinking about that. Did you notice how when we last came back from 1940, we thought we'd been gone at least an hour, but when we came back your mom said it was only five minutes?'

'And five minutes was about the time it took us to get to the shelter and back,' said Jack.

'Right,' said Ella. 'I think it's possible the shelter took us back from 1940, right to the same moment we left.'

'You mean it's like we never went away?' said Jack.

'Exactly. So we can probably go back to 1940 even for a couple of days, and nobody will know because we'll come back at the same time we left.'

'Wow,' said Jack. 'You could be right. It's worth a

try anyway. Let's start packing stuff for the journey.'

'Good idea,' said Ella. 'But aren't you forgetting something Jack? You're supposed to be cleaning your room.'

'You said you'd help me,' said Jack.

'No I didn't,' said Ella, laughing. 'I just told Aunt Claire I'd make sure you cleaned up.'

'You're so bossy,' grumbled Jack. He bundled up all his clothes and books from the floor into one big heap, and shoved them into the wardrobe. 'That OK?' he asked.

'I guess that will have to do!' laughed Ella.

Jack and Ella spent the next two days in eager anticipation of their next trip back in time. Because it was the weekend, Mr and Mrs Thomas took them to some places of interest in London that Ella had not seen before. Try as she might, Ella could not stop thinking about the shelter, even when they were doing things she would normally have found exciting, like travelling up into the air on the big ferris wheel known as the London Eye. Just to be polite, she made a little video on her phone of the buildings and roads of London spread out below them.

Finally, Monday came. Jack and Ella whispered to each other excitedly as they walked out into the garden after breakfast.

'All set?' asked Jack.

'Sure, I'm ready,' said Ella. She noticed Jack's small backpack. 'What's in your bag?'

'Oh, just some drinks and snacks and stuff in case we get hungry,' he said. 'Mum won't mind us taking them. I also put a newspaper in there.'

'Why?' said Ella. 'Who wants to read a boring newspaper?'

'Not to read, silly,' said Jack. 'It's to prove we come from the future.'

'Hey, great idea,' said Ella with a grin. 'Come on, let's get going.'

Once again the two children squeezed through the gap in the fence and crept through the undergrowth to the shelter. They hurried inside and crouched down at the back of the small, dark space and watched through the little doorway.

'Do you hear anything?' whispered Ella. 'Are we starting to go back through time yet?'

'Shh!' said Jack. 'I think…' Before Jack could finish there was an enormous crash and a hot blast of air shot through the doorway.

'It's happened again!' said Jack excitedly. He realised that he could not hear anything except for a loud wailing noise. He waggled his fingers in his ears but the sound did not go away. He noticed Ella was doing the same.

'What the heck is that noise?' said Ella.

'I remember now,' said Jack. 'Peter told us it was the all-clear. That means the bomber planes have gone.'

They peeked out of the doorway of the shelter and, once again, saw that the overgrown jungle of the garden had changed back to the neat lawn and flower beds of 1940.

'What do we do now?' said Ella.

'We need to find Peter,' said Jack. 'After all, if

we're going to go exploring in 1940, we're going to need someone friendly to show us around.'

'You're right,' said Ella. 'There's going to be all kinds of stuff we don't understand.'

'Like what?' asked Jack.

'Like, I don't know, how to use a telephone or turn on the TV.'

'We don't need to use a telephone and I don't even think they had TV back then,' said Jack.

'OK then,' said Ella. 'I mean stuff like how to use the bathroom.'

'I don't think *that's* changed,' said Jack with a giggle. 'Anyway,' he continued, 'let's try to find Peter.'

They stepped out of the shelter and looked around them. There was a smell of smoke in the air again, and in the distance they could hear alarm bells ringing. Beyond the nearby railway line there was a large cloud of black smoke rising up into the air.

They crept to the gap in the hedge and looked out at Peter's house. It looked empty, and Peter was nowhere to be seen. Suddenly, a figure leapt out in front of them from the side of the hedge.

Chapter Nine
Captured by the Police

Jack and Ella jumped back in surprise. It was Peter.

'Hullo,' he said. You here again?'

'Oh, er, hi Peter,' said Jack. 'Where were you?'

'In the house, waiting for the all-clear, of course. What happened to you?' asked Peter. 'You disappeared into thin air.'

'What do you mean?' asked Ella.

'After that big raid a few days ago. I came out after the all-clear to see you again but you'd disappeared. So I wondered if you might use this shelter again and sure enough you did.'

'Er, we had to get back home,' said Jack. Ella nodded in agreement. She noticed that this time, Peter had a little cardboard box tied round his shoulder with string, and wondered what on earth it could be.

'Hmm, that reminds me,' said Peter. He looked at them suspiciously. 'Just where do you live, exactly?'

Ella tried to sound casual. 'Oh, we're just here on vacation. Er, I mean, holiday. From the United States.'

'I know, you said that before,' said Peter. 'But where are you staying around here? Nearly all the children in London have been evacuated. And I've never heard of Americans coming here on holiday during wartime.' He pointed to Jack. 'And *you're* not American. You sound English.'

Peter moved closer to them and continued talking. He seemed to be becoming more suspicious. 'Then there's your odd clothes. And why haven't you got gas masks?'

'Gas masks?' asked Ella. 'Why do we need those?'

'That's just what I mean,' said Peter. 'Everyone knows he has to carry a gas mask at all times, in case the Germans drop poison gas on us. Like this one.'

He opened the little cardboard box which was slung around his shoulder with string. Inside was a sinister looking black mask with round eyeholes and a nose like a big salt shaker.

'Oh, erm, we must have lost them,' said Ella.

'Ella,' said Jack. 'I think we should tell Peter the truth.'

Peter started walking towards Jack and Ella; they backed slowly towards the shelter.

'Yes, I think you ought to tell me the truth,' said Peter. 'This is all a bit suspicious,' he continued. 'You turn up from nowhere wearing odd clothes, and don't seem to know anything about what's going on. Maybe Mrs Simpson was right about you two.'

'Mrs...Simpson?' asked Ella.

'She's the old lady next door,' said Peter. 'The one you spoke to. She came round and asked mother who you were and why I was talking to you. She thinks you might be spies.'

'Spies!' said Jack. 'But that's crazy!'

'Well, Mrs Simpson is a bit peculiar, I agree,' said Peter. 'But look here. Just tell me where you live, to make sure.'

'I've told you, we live next door!' said Jack. He was starting to get angry about all these questions.

'Mrs Simpson's never seen you before, so you can't live next door,' said Peter. 'Come on, out with it.'

'OK, Peter,' said Ella. She took a deep breath. 'We come from the future.'

Peter looked puzzled. 'From the future? Don't talk such rot!' He looked very angry now. 'Right, that's it.' He turned to go.

'Where are you going?' asked Jack.

'I'm going to tell mother to telephone the police. I think you *are* spies. Or at the very least, some sort of runaways.'

Before they could speak, Peter turned on his heels and started walking briskly away across the garden. 'Peter, wait,' shouted Jack. 'We really do come from the future. Look, I can prove it to you.'

Jack sprinted after Peter and stopped in front of him. He was a little nervous as Peter was bigger than him and he didn't want to get in a fight with him.

'Alright, how?' said Peter with a sigh.

'Look at this. It's a newspaper. From the future.' Jack took out the paper from his backpack and showed it to Peter. He pointed to the front page. 'Look at the date.'

'Hmm,' said Peter. 'That doesn't prove anything. You could have had that made by a local printer.'

'Oh come on,' said Jack. 'Why would we do that?'
Suddenly from behind them the boys heard their own voices repeated back to them.

'What on earth...?' said Peter, turning round.

Ella stood in front of them. She was holding up her phone and on the screen a video was playing of the boys talking.

'I just filmed you,' said Ella. 'And now I'm playing it back to you. I bet you've never seen anything like this before.'

Peter craned forward to peer at the little screen. 'Rather!' I've never seen anything like it. Is it a cine camera, or is it television? '

'So you know about TV, er, I mean, television?' said Jack.

'Of course. But only a few people have it because it's awfully expensive. And they stopped all the broadcasts when the war started. So that little thing of Ella's can't possibly be a television.'

Ella laughed. 'It's not TV. It's a phone. But it can make videos...erm, I guess you call them movies, and all kinds of other cool stuff. '

'But...but this is amazing,' said Peter.

'Now do you believe we're from the future?' asked Jack.

'I should say so,' said Peter enthusiastically. 'It's like that film I was telling you about. *Buck Rogers.* He went forward in time rather than back of course, but still, it's the same sort of thing.'

Peter looked around the garden. 'Let's get into the shelter,' he said. 'I'd rather mother didn't see you out here. I've all sorts of things to ask you.'

They trooped into the shelter, sat on the bottom bunk and shared out the snacks which Jack had brought. Peter munched enthusiastically on a chocolate bar.

'I haven't had chocolate this good for ages,' he said. 'It's all rationed now so I don't get sweets that often.'

Between bites Peter asked all sorts of questions about the future. Jack and Ella did their best to answer them. He seemed very interested in technology and was intrigued by the camera on Ella's phone. Unfortunately they found that the videos and pictures that Ella had taken previously did not work, for some reason, but they were still able to take photos and videos of each other.

'I like taking photographs,' said Peter, 'but I've only got a Box Brownie.'

'What's that?' asked Jack.

'It's a camera,' replied Peter. 'I'll get it and show you later.'

'I should have brought my tablet,' said Jack.

'Why?' asked Peter. 'Are you ill?'

'No,' said Jack. 'I don't mean that sort of tablet. It's a kind of computer.'

'Gosh,' said Peter. 'I've read about computers as well. Turing Machines, they call them. But they've only made one or two. And to think I've met someone who owns one!'

After asking lots more questions, Peter suddenly fell silent for a moment.

'What's the matter?' asked Ella.

'I just had a thought,' said Peter. 'I can't believe I didn't ask this before. If you really do come from the future, I suppose...you must know who wins the war.'

'Sure,' said Ella. 'Don't worry. Britain wins. And America.'

'That's super!' yelled Peter, and then lowered his voice in case anybody heard them. 'And it's super that America joins in. Father said they would eventually, and then we'd win.'

'Bad news though,' said Jack. 'You'll have to wait a while. The war ended in 1945.'

'Oh Lord,' said Peter. 'Five years. That's an awfully long time to wait. I'll be *sixteen.* And I probably won't get to see father all that time.' Peter looked down at his shoes and sniffed. Ella wondered if he was going to start crying.

'Why won't you see your dad?' she asked.

'He's a prisoner of war,' said Peter quietly. 'He was in the army and got captured at Dunkirk a few months ago. That's in France. Now all we know is he's in a prison somewhere in Germany. That's why mother got so lonely and asked me to come back for the summer hols.'

Ella tried to reassure Peter. 'Never mind, I guess he'll be OK. They'll have to let him go when the war ends.'

Peter sniffed again then smiled. 'Yes, I suppose you're right. We can't feel sorry for ourselves, can we? Keep calm and carry on, that's what the poster says.'

'Hey, my mum's got that poster on the wall above her desk,' said Jack. 'I never knew that was from the war.'

'Something else has occurred to me,' said Peter.

'How on earth are you going to get back to your own time?'

'We've thought of that,' said Ella. 'Jack and I talked to our uncle, who's some kind of professor and really smart. He said it could be possible to travel through time if there was a really big explosion. Something to do with some guy called Einstein.'

'Of course,' said Peter. 'Albert Einstein. I've heard about him. He's come up with all sorts of theories about time travel.'

'Right,' said Ella. 'Anyway, me and Jack guessed that the shelter only travels through time when a bomb goes off nearby. So we found out the dates of all the bomb raids on this part of London on a website.'

'What's a website?' asked Peter.

Jack struggled to explain. 'It's, well, it's information on a computer.'

'Go on,' said Peter, nodding.

Jack continued. 'So we found out the next air raid is on Monday. As long as we're in here when it happens, we should be able to go back to our own time.'

'I say,' said Peter. 'That's awfully clever. It's Saturday today, so that gives us today and tomorrow together.'

'Yes,' said Ella. 'So we definitely want to check out what London was like in 1940. Do you think you can show us around?'

'I'd love to,' said Peter. 'Oh…but I think you're going to need some new clothes. Those ones you're wearing might attract attention.'

'Really?' asked Ella, looking down at her purple hoodie and leggings, and Jack's tee shirt and cargo pants. 'You mean people don't wear stuff like this?'

'No,' said Peter. 'Nor like Jack's clothes either. Tell you what. Mother has a bag of old clothes she's collecting to help war refugees. Some of my old stuff's in there and that will fit Jack. I think she got some stuff from the family over the road as well, and there's a girl about your age there. Anyway, give me two ticks and we'll find out. I'll fetch my Box Brownie and show you that as well.'

While they waited they heard a noise at the back of the house next door. Ella looked up out of the shelter to see the old lady, Mrs Simpson, glaring at her as she closed her window. Ella glared back and the lady disappeared back into the room.

A few minutes later Peter re-appeared with an old sack. He rummaged through it and took out a tweed skirt, a ladies' blouse and pullover, and some shoes.

'Here you are,' he said, giving the clothes to Ella. 'See if these fit.'

Ella waited. 'What?' said Peter.

'Er, how about some privacy?' said Ella.

Peter blushed. 'Oh, sorry. Come on Jack, we'll wait outside.'

The boys waited outside the shelter while Ella changed. The clothes were a little big for her but by rolling up the jumper sleeves she managed to make herself look quite presentable, although it was hard to tell as there was no mirror in the shelter.

She stepped outside. 'These clothes feel weird,' said Ella. 'Even my grandma wouldn't wear something like this. And these shoes are way too big.' She wiggled her finger around her heel to show a big gap between it and the shoe.

'I think you look perfectly alright,' said Peter. 'And we can soon make those shoes fit. Here, try this.'

Peter went into the shelter and emerged with a newspaper from the small pile by the bunk beds. He tore off a piece and scrunched it into a ball.

'Give me the shoes,' he said. Ella took them off and gave them to him. He pushed the scrunched up paper down into the shoes and gave them back. 'Now try them.'

'Weird,' said Ella, shaking her head. She tried on the shoes again. 'I guess they're OK,' she said, doubtfully.

'Well they'll just have to do,' said Peter. '"Make do and mend", that's what mother keeps saying. Now you try some of my old togs on, Jack.'

'OK,' said Jack. He stepped into the shelter and a few minutes later emerged wearing similar clothes to Peter – brown shoes with long grey socks pulled up to his knees, baggy shorts, a white shirt and a green sleeveless pullover.

'This alright? he asked.

Ella laughed. 'Cool,' she said. 'You look pretty much like Peter now.'

'I shouldn't wonder,' said Peter. 'He's wearing my clothes. Well, nobody would give you a second glance now.'

'Great,' said Jack. 'So let's start exploring!'

'Rather!' said Peter. 'but first let me take a picture of you two.'

Jack and Ella stood outside the shelter while Peter made some adjustments to his camera. He looked through a little hole in the top and then pushed a button.

'All done,' he said, putting the camera into the shelter. 'I say, do either of you have any money?'

'No,' said Jack. 'We didn't bring any.'

'Hmm, probably just as well,' said Peter. 'People might get suspicious if you started using coins with dates from years in the future on them. Never mind. I've got some of my pocket money saved up. Enough to buy us all a bus ticket into central London. Come on!'

'We can go on our own?' said Jack.

'Of course,' said Peter. 'We're not babies!'

'It's just that in our time, kids don't really get to go around much on their own,' said Ella.

'That's rotten luck,' said Peter. 'The only problem we might have though is somebody might ask why we haven't been evacuated. Hopefully nobody will but if they do, don't say anything. "Careless talk costs lives" – that's another poster I've seen that says that.'

'OK,' said Ella. 'We'll keep quiet.'

'Come on then,' said Peter. 'The bus stop's just down the road.'

The three children crossed the lawn and were about to leave by the side gate. Just as Peter was about to open it, the kitchen door opened and a lady in a floral dress and apron appeared.

'Peter, where are you going?' she demanded. 'And who are these children?'

'Oh, hullo mother,' said Peter, as casually as he could. 'We're just off for a trip on the bus. Don't mind, do you?'

Peter's mother – Mrs Bennett – frowned. 'Yes I do rather. I'd like you to introduce me to your two friends first,' she said.

'They're called Jack and Ella,' said Peter. He stepped forward to the gate. 'Must dash. Cheerio!'

'Not so fast young man,' said Mrs Bennett, putting her hand on the latch of the gate. 'There's someone inside who would like a word with "Jack" and "Ella", if indeed those are your names.'

Mrs Bennett stepped out of the way and a tall figure wearing a dark uniform and a round helmet stepped into the garden. It was the policeman who had seen them in the road before.

'Now then,' said the policeman in a very serious voice. 'We've had a complaint from one of the neighbours. The lady next door said that you,' – he pointed to Ella with a large, bony finger – 'tried to force your way into her house a couple of days ago.'

'I didn't!' cried Ella. 'I was just trying to….'

'That's enough from you just now, young lady,' said the policeman. 'I ask the questions around here, and first I'd like to find out just exactly who you two are and where you come from.'

Chapter Ten
Meet Mrs Murgatroyd

'Now come along,' said the policeman. 'I want your full names and addresses. And don't start thinking of making them up, as I can always check.' He unbuttoned a pocket on his jacket and took out a notepad and pencil.

'My name's Jack Thomas,' said Jack, 'and this is my cousin Ella, erm, Ella Riley. We don't live around here…at the moment.'

'I see,' said the policeman. 'And where *do* you live? I don't think I've seen you on my beat before, and anyway, all children are supposed to have left London for the evacuation.'

'We're really sorry to have caused any trouble, officer,' said Ella. 'We didn't meant to. And we can't tell you our addresses, because….because…we come from the future!'

'Now you've torn it,' said Peter.

'Quiet!' hissed Mrs Bennett.

The policeman sighed. 'Don't you know there's a war on? I haven't got time to play silly games with children. For the last time, where do you live?'

'It's true,' said Jack. 'We do come from the future, and we can prove it. Ella, show him your phone.'

Ella's face brightened. 'Great idea.' She took out the phone, which she had been keeping in the pocket of her skirt.

'Just a moment, if you don't mind, young lady,' said the policeman. 'I'll take charge of that. It could be a weapon for all I know.' He deftly removed the phone from Ella's hand.

'Hmm,' said the policeman, turning over the phone in his hand. 'I don't know what this is exactly, but I'll wager it's some sort of cigarette case or make-up box.'

'It's not,' said Peter. 'It's a sort of pocket camera that makes and plays films, and does all sorts of other things. They showed me earlier. I'm pretty sure Jack and Ella *are* from the future as I've never seen anything like that before. They said they travelled through time in the Anderson shelter and I believe them.'

'Don't talk such nonsense Peter,' said Mrs Bennett. 'You must stop making up stories and getting people into trouble.'

'Just a minute, young man,' said the policeman, turning to Peter. 'I'm not interested in fairy tales about travelling through time, but did you just say this little gadget could make and show cine films?'

'Yes,' said Peter defiantly. 'It's technology from the future.'

'Now listen to me very carefully,' said the policeman, turning back to Jack and Ella. He pointed to the phone in his hand. 'You need to tell me where you got this thing. We've reason to believe there are fifth columnists – that's another name for spies –

who are going around taking cine films of airfields and other defences, to send back to Germany. We know they've got lots of clever little gadgets. So unless you tell me this instant where you got this, I'm going to have to take you to the police station and you'll be in very serious trouble.'

'You've got to believe us,' said Ella. 'That's not a spy camera. It's a phone, from the future. Please let me have it back and I'll prove it to you.'

The policeman looked at Ella suspiciously. 'Alright, young lady. But this is your last warning.' He handed back the phone.

Ella pushed the 'on' button. Nothing happened. She pushed it again, harder. Still nothing.

'Oh,' she said, in a small voice. 'We must have run down the battery when we were showing Peter all those videos and stuff. And I don't have a charger.'

'It doesn't matter,' said Jack. 'I've brought a newspaper from the future. And clothes, too. They're in the shelter in my backpack. I'll get it and prove everything to you.' He turned away from the policeman who stepped forward and blocked his path into the garden.

'Oh no you don't, sonny,' said the policeman. 'That's enough silly games for today. You two are coming with me.'

From behind him, Jack heard Ella shout. 'Quick Jack, run!'

Before he had a chance to think, he spun round and saw Ella sprinting through the side gate. Peter and Mrs Bennett leapt back in surprise into the kitchen.

Jack followed and careered round the side of the house behind Ella. They heard the policeman shout something to Mrs Bennett, and then a loud beeping noise as he blew a whistle to summon help.

Jack felt his heart pounding in his chest as he raced along the pavement for several minutes; he soon caught up with Ella. She turned to him and shouted 'Jack, I can't run in these shoes, they're too big for me!'

Almost as soon as she had spoken, she tripped over and sprawled on the pavement. 'Ow!' she cried, clutching her knee.

Jack stopped and tried to help, but it was no use. As he turned to look behind him, he saw the dark shape of the policeman looming over him, and then felt a big hand grasp the back of his pullover and pull him upright. The policeman then helped Ella up and plonked both of them on a nearby garden wall. He held firmly on to both of them.

'You two are most definitely in trouble,' he said. 'Running away from a policeman who orders you to stop is very serious. I told Mrs Bennett to dial 999 on the telephone, and they'll be a police car round here any minute. We're going to get to the bottom of all this.'

As he was speaking, the sound of an electric bell could be heard ringing in the distance. A large, very old-fashioned black car with 'POLICE' painted in white letters on the side turned the corner into Cotswold Avenue. The car stopped by the policeman and the bell stopped ringing.

'Cor, Bert,' said the driver, with a grin. 'Are these

the two German spies then? That's what the lady on the telephone said, according to the radio in here. Good job we were just passing or they might have escaped in a submarine up the canal.'

Ella didn't think it was funny. 'We're not spies!' she said angrily. 'And I'm American'.

''Course you are my little darling,' said the driver, as he got out of the car and opened the back door. 'And I'm the Queen of Sheba.'

'What's he talking about?' asked Jack.

'Come along, in you get,' said the policeman, and bundled Jack and Ella into the back seat of the car. It had dark brown seats made of some sort of leathery material, and smelled of petrol and cigarette smoke.

The policeman slammed the door shut and got into the front seat next to the driver. There was the sound of gears crunching and then the car sped off. Jack and Ella looked out of the windows with astonishment as the car weaved through the busy traffic of suburban London. It was like watching an old film, except that it was real. They saw people in old fashioned clothes and hats, and funny looking old cars, and even one or two horses and carts.

The shops all looked as if they were something in a museum display. Everywhere they looked there was evidence of the war; they saw houses that had been completely destroyed by bombs and even saw a group of soldiers marching along the road.

After about ten minutes the car pulled into a yard behind a building near a park. Jack looked up to see a blue lamp outside the door with 'POLICE' painted on it in white letters.

'Hey,' said Jack. 'I know this place. It's the old Northgate police station.'

'Nothing old about this place,' said the driver with a chuckle. 'Only built a few years ago.'

'Come on, out you get,' said the policeman. Jack and Ella stepped out of the car and the policeman led them up some steps into a big hallway with dark wooden benches on them. At the end of the hallway was a big desk, and a policeman with three white stripes on each arm sat writing in a big book. As Jack and Ella approached him he looked up.

'Afternoon, Henderson,' said the man. 'These your two spies then? I hope they didn't put up too much of a fight.'

'Afternoon, sergeant,' said the policeman. 'They're runaways, I think. We'll do the usual with them.'

Jack swallowed hard and wondered what 'the usual' meant.

'What do you think's going to happen to us?' whispered Ella to Jack.

'No talking,' said the policeman sternly, and led them into a small office. He pointed to a wooden bench by a desk and they sat down on it.

The policeman took his helmet off and placed it on the desk. He sat down and looked at Jack and Ella.

'Turn your pockets out,' he said.

Jack didn't have anything in his pockets and Ella only had her phone, which she put on the desk.

'Now you two,' said the policeman, 'don't look so frightened. I don't think you're spies – I'm pretty sure the Germans aren't sending ten year olds out to do their dirty work.'

'We're both eleven, sir,' said Jack.

'Then starting acting a bit more grown up, lad,' said the policeman. 'And you don't have to call me sir. You can call me PC Henderson.'

'What are you going to do with us?' said Ella.

'What I should do is get the army involved and give them this little gadget here.'

'You mean my phone?' said Ella. 'But, but you can't, it was a present from my mom and dad.'

'Alright, alright, calm down,' said PC Henderson, raising his hand. 'I'm going to let you keep that, whatever it is I don't think it's a German spy camera.' He handed the phone back to Ella. 'But what I am going to do is get Mrs Murgatroyd to collect you.'

'Who's Mrs Murgatroyd?' asked Jack.

'She's the person we call when we find runaways,'

'But we haven't run away from anywhere,' said Ella.

'So you say young lady,' said PC Henderson. 'But we don't know who you are. All you've given me is some silly story about travelling through time. Well I don't believe it. I think you've been evacuated and you've run away and come back to London.'

'We haven't, honestly,' said Jack.

'I don't want any more fibbing,' said PC Henderson. 'It's not up to me anymore. You're not the first ones you know.'

'The first what?' asked Ella.

'Runaways,' said PC Henderson. 'We've already picked up a few. Some of them didn't like the places they got evacuated to in the country, and managed to get back to London. Now, we don't mind that so much because if their parents agreed to it there's nothing we can do. But some of these children were orphans. They lived in a children's home and got evacuated to the country, but then ran away. I've got a feeling that's what you two are. Aren't you? This is your last chance to tell me.'

'No,' said Jack. 'We've already told you where we come from but you didn't believe us.'

'Alright,' said PC Henderson with a sigh. 'You leave me no choice. I'll have to telephone Mrs Murgatroyd. She'll come and collect you.'

'What…what will happen to us?' said Ella.

'Don't look so terrified,' said PC Henderson. 'She won't eat you. She'll check her records to see if you match the descriptions of any recent runaways.'

'But there won't be any records of us,' said Jack.

PC Henderson smiled. 'I know, because you come from the planet Mars in the year two-thousand. Alright then, have it your own way. If Mrs Murgatroyd can't find any records of you, you'll be placed in an orphanage out in the country.' He picked up an old black telephone on the desk and spoke into it.

'Put me through to Mrs Murgatroyd please. District Welfare Officer. Yes, that's right.'

After a few seconds' pause, PC Henderson spoke again. 'Good afternoon Mrs Murgatroyd. It's Fred Henderson here at Northgate police station. Yes, quite well thank you. I've got another couple of runaways for you. Boy and a girl. Their names? Just a moment.'

PC Henderson took his notebook out of his top pocked and looked inside it.

'Their names are Jack Thomas and Ella Riley. Both aged approximately eleven. No identity papers and refusing to tell us anything.'

There was another pause and then PC Henderson spoke again. 'I see, yes, well thank you. We'll expect you shortly. Yes, good day to you, ma'am.' He replaced the receiver and folded his arms.

'Well you two, it seems there's been no reports of any runaways of your description lately.'

'Great,' said Ella. 'So can we please go now?'

'No you may not, young lady,' said PC Henderson. 'Mrs Murgatroyd is going to come and collect you.'

'But...but where will she take us?' asked Jack.

'Like I said, most likely to one of the orphanages set up in the country. If at any time you decide to start talking sense, you'll be put back in the care of your parents.'

Ella sniffed and looked as if she was going to start crying. Jack just looked down at his shoes.

'Now, now,' said PC Henderson. 'Don't take on. They're not such bad places, these children's homes. At least you'll be away from the bombs. Us grown-ups have to stay here and put up with them. How about a glass of lemonade?'

Both Jack and Ella realised they had not had anything to eat or drink for a while.

'Yes please,' they said in unison.

PC Henderson smiled. The children had not seen him do that before. It made him look much less scary.

'Right you are then,' he said. 'Two lemonades coming up. And I'll see if there's anyone in the canteen willing to give up his biscuit ration.'

A few minutes later Jack and Ella were slurping glasses of lemonade and eating biscuits as they waited for Mrs Murgatroyd to arrive.

'I envy you children, getting away to the countryside,' said PC Henderson. 'Can't think why you'd want to run back to London. You won't want to be here soon.'

'Why not? asked Jack.

'If you think the bombing's bad now, wait a few weeks. Jerry – or to use the proper title, the German air force – is trying to knock out our defences and they'll keep at it until they do.'

'What will happen then?' asked Ella.

'There'll be an invasion, most likely,' said PC Henderson. '"We will fight them in the streets", as the prime minister says. So you're best out of it.'

'Will you have to join the army?' said Jack.

'I tried to,' said PC Henderson, 'but they said I was too old and so I had to stay in the police. But we're ready if there's an invasion.'

'What do you mean? Asked Ella.

'Everyone thinks the British bobby doesn't carry a gun,' said PC Henderson, 'but have a look at this.'

He walked over to a metal cupboard and unlocked it. Inside was a row of guns. He took out a rifle.

'See this,' he said, holding the rifle up to his shoulder and pointing it through the window. 'This is called a Ross Rifle. The Canadians sent us a whole lot of them. And if Jerry tries to invade London we'll be there to stop him.'

'Cool,' said Jack. 'I hope we get to s

'No you don't, son,' said PC Hend
his head sadly. He put the rifle back i
and locked it. 'There's nothing excit
Believe me, I fought in the one bef
wouldn't wish that on anyone.'

Just then there was a knock on the door and the
sergeant from the front desk came in.

'Mrs Murgatroyd's here,' said the sergeant.

'Right-oh,' said PC Henderson. He turned to Jack
and Ella. 'I'll say goodbye now. I'll put in a good
word for you with the welfare office but I suggest
you stop fibbing about where you come from as soon
as possible. '

He walked out and closed the door. Jack and Ella
could hear him talking with a lady outside the room.
She sounded quite angry. Ella looked at Jack with a
worried expression on her face. She had just noticed
the date on a calendar on the desk: Saturday 17th
August 1940.

'Jack, we can't stay away from the shelter too long,'
she whispered. 'We've got to be there on Wednesday
19th, to get back to our own time.'

'I know,' said Jack. 'Let's hope we don't have to
stay with this Mrs Mur…wotsit that long.'

Before they could say anything else, the door burst
open and a large lady in a dark blue uniform with a
blue hat walked briskly in. She was very ugly, with a
large nose, curly grey hair and several warts on her
face. She clapped her hands together twice.

'Now then, stand up. Up!'

and Ella looked at each other, then stood up.

'My name is Murgatroyd, Mrs Murgatroyd. District Welfare Officer for evacuees. Stand up straight. Take your hands out of your pockets, boy.'

Jack took his hands out of his pockets and held them by his sides. Ella gave Jack a shocked look.

'And don't roll your eyes, girl,' said Mrs Murgatroyd. 'If the wind changes your face will stay that way.'

'Erm, ma'am, can we talk to you about something?' said Ella in a hesitant voice.

'Silence,' snapped Mrs Murgatroyd. 'Don't speak until you're spoken to. Now listen to me. You've put the authorities to a great deal of trouble. We have better things to do than chase ungrateful runaways. Get your gas masks and come with me.'

'Please miss,' said Jack. 'We don't have any gas masks,'

'Typical,' said Mrs Murgatroyd, with a sharp intake of breath. 'Those masks were provided at public expense for your protection, but you threw them away.'

'We didn't,' said Ella angrily. 'We never had any.'

'That's enough from you,' said Mrs Murgatroyd. 'I've heard from PC Henderson that you made up a nonsensical story about coming from the future or something. *He* seems to think you might have been psychologically damaged by an air raid.'

'You mean he thinks we're crazy?' said Ella.

'To put it bluntly, yes,' said Mrs Murgatroyd. 'Well that won't wash with me. You're coming with me now to an evacuation centre, and tomorrow we will

112

go by train to an orphanage in the country.'

'How long for?' asked Jack.

'For at least a week,' said Mrs Murgatroyd. 'That will give us long enough to find out who you *really* are. Now, wait here until I bring my motor car to the front door. We're not risking you running away again.'

Mrs Murgatroyd turned on her heel and Jack and Ella were left alone in the room.

'A week!' wailed Ella. 'That means we won't be able to get back the shelter.'

Jack nodded grimly. 'And that means we'll never get back to our own time.'

Chapter Eleven
Evacuated

The two children stared glumly out of the windows of Mrs Murgatroyd's car as she drove through London. The excitement they had first felt on arriving in the 1940s had begun to wear off, and they were scared about what might be in store for them.

'She's gross, that lady,' whispered Ella to Jack. 'Mrs Whatshername. I can't even remember how to say it.'

'It's Mrs…Mur something. Murder Droid!'

Ella started giggling. 'That's so funny. That suits her totally. The Murder Droid!'

They both began laughing until Mrs Murgatroyd turned round to look at them, while the car was stopped at a junction.

'That's enough of that,' she said. 'I don't want any distractions while I'm driving. You will remain quiet.'

Jack and Ella struggled to stop giggling, and eventually they managed to keep quiet. At the next junction, the car slowed down and Ella noticed that instead of traffic lights, a policeman wearing white gloves was controlling the flow of cars.

'Jack, look,' whispered Ella. 'There's a policeman. What if we shouted for help and told him we'd been kidnapped? Then we might be able to get away.'

'No,' said Jack, shaking his head. 'I don't think that would do any good. We'd probably just get caught again and be in even worse trouble.'

Mrs Murgatroyd looked round again. 'I shan't tell you again. Absolute silence.'

Jack and Ella both sighed and looked out of the window. They were now passing through a built-up part of London, and there was much more damage here from bombs than in Northgate. They saw some odd sights, such as a house where one wall had completely disappeared, allowing everyone to see the furniture and wallpaper inside, as if it were a giant doll's house that somebody had just opened.

Eventually the car stopped outside a church hall.

'Out,' said Mrs Murgatroyd. Jack and Ella stepped out on to the pavement. Before they could even think about running away, Mrs Murgatroyd took Jack and Ella's hands in a vice-like grip, and both children shuddered as they felt her clammy skin in contact with theirs.

They walked into the church hall which had several camp beds in rows along the walls, and a number of children were sitting around reading or playing board games. Nobody paid much attention to Jack and Ella.

'This is the reception centre,' said Mrs Murgatroyd proudly. 'You will be held here until tomorrow, and then we shall travel by train to the orphanage.'

115

'But…' began Ella.

'No "buts"', snapped Mrs Murgatroyd. 'Boys on one side, girls on the other. There are two free beds left. We shall see if we can find some night clothes for you. You've missed lunch, but it will be supper and then lights out shortly.'

Mrs Murgatroyd noticed Ella glancing towards the door of the church hall.

'Don't get any ideas about running away, young lady,' she said. 'Those doors are kept locked at all times.' To illustrate her point, she took out a large key chain from her skirt pocket, walked over to the doors and locked them with a noisy clatter of metal.

Jack and Ella sat down on their little camp beds on opposite sides of the hall, while Mrs Murgatroyd disappeared into a room at the far end of the hall.

A small boy with tousled hair and round glasses mended with tape, who was lying on one of the beds, put his book down and looked at Jack and Ella.

'Hullo you two,' he said. 'My name's Tom. What's yours?'

Jack and Ella introduced themselves and Tom lay back on his bed. 'You've met Goering then,' he said.

'Who?' asked Ella.

'Goering. You know, the big fat German fellow in charge of their air force. He's always appearing in the newsreels shouting orders at people. It's what we call Mrs Murgatroyd. Sort of a joke name.'

'Oh right,' said Jack. 'We call her the Murder Droid.'

'What does that mean?' asked Tom.

'Never mind,' sighed Ella. 'It's kind of hard to

explain. I guess you don't have droids here.'

'Never heard of them,' said Tom. 'Anyway, what are you in here for?'

Jack and Ella looked at each other. Ella shook her head and Jack took that to mean that they should not tell Tom that they had come for the future.

'We're runaways,' said Jack. 'We're both from, erm, a long way off.'

'A very long way,' said Ella. 'Jack's my cousin and I came to visit him. I'm from the USA. So don't be surprised if we don't know a lot of stuff like who Goering is or stuff about the war.'

'Alright,' said Tom with a shrug. 'Just wondering.'

'Why are *you* here?' asked Jack.

'Well...' began Tom, who suddenly looked very sad. 'My mum got killed in an air raid. I was supposed to be evacuated but mum didn't want me to go. Our house got hit by a bomb, I was alright but mum didn't make it. Now I have to go and live in that orphanage place.'

Ella swallowed hard. 'That's terrible,' she said. 'But couldn't your dad look after you?'

'He's dead too,' said Tom. 'He was in the army and got killed in France. I don't have any aunts or uncles or anything, at least nobody who knows me well enough to look after me.'

'That's awful,' said Jack.

'Not much I can do about it really,' said Tom with a shrug. 'Just got to carry on. Most of us are in here for the same reason.' He turned his head away from them, took his glasses off and rubbed them on his handkerchief.

Ella felt a tug at her sleeve. She looked round to see a small girl in a flowery dress and cardigan looking at her with an admiring expression.

'I heard you talking,' said the girl. 'Are you really runaways?'

'Erm, I guess,' said Ella. 'We ran away from the police but they caught us and took us to the police department.'

'It sounds scary,' said the girl, looking at Ella with wide eyes.

'It was pretty much OK really,' said Ella with a shrug. 'They gave us soda and cookies and we got to look at some guns.'

'Gosh,' said the girl. 'It sounds exciting. I'm only here because my mother's had to go into hospital for a while. I've heard some children run away from where they were evacuated to, because the people they had to stay with were horrid. But I've never met any.'

'Well now you have,' said Jack. 'And we're going to do it again.'

The little girl's eyes widened even more. 'Really?' she said, 'but why? Were the people who looked after you very mean?'

'No, it's not that,' said Ella. 'It's just we don't, well, we don't really belong here. We've got to get back home.'

Tom put his glasses back on and looked round the room, checking that no grown-ups were about. The other children in the hall were talking or playing in small groups and not paying them any attention.

'Are you really going to run away?' asked Tom in a

whisper.

'I think so,' said Ella.

'But the doors are locked,' said Jack. 'How are we going to do it?'

'Goering keeps the front door locked,' said Tom, 'but there's another way out, through the kitchen, back there.' He pointed to the door at the end of the hall that Mrs Murgatroyd had disappeared into.

'I reckon all you need to do,' continued Tom, 'is wait for the grown ups to leave that room after supper's over. Then after lights out, you can creep in there and go out through the back door.'

'But how do you know they don't lock the back door too?' asked Ella.

'They do, but they keep the key in the lock,' said Tom. 'I saw it this afternoon when we went in to get our lunch.'

'I don't like the sound of this,' said Jack. 'How are we going to get back to Northgate in the middle of the night?'

'We'll figure something out,' said Ella. 'This could be our only chance. Once they take us a long way away from the shelter, we might never get back.'

'Alright,' said Jack. 'It's on.'

'An escape!' said Tom, with a big grin on his face. 'It's like we're in a prison camp and Goering is the chief guard!'

Tom and the little girl started laughing and Jack and Ella couldn't help joining in, even though both of them were worried about the thought of escaping into the night, with no way of knowing how to get back to the air raid shelter at Peter's house.

Just then a lady came out of the door at the back of the hall and approached them. She was wearing the same blue uniform as Mrs Murgatroyd, with a small badge on her chest which read 'Womens' Voluntary Service.' But unlike Mrs Murgatroyd, this lady was small and thin. She wore round spectacles and looked nervous.

'You'll be the two new arrivals, I expect,' she said . 'You're Jack and Ella, aren't you?'

Jack and Ella nodded. 'Very well,' continued the lady. 'I'm Miss Withers, I'm Mrs Murgatroyd's second-in-command. I've bought these night clothes for you. Don't worry, they've been washed and ironed.'

She handed some striped pyjamas to Jack and a cotton nightdress to Ella.

'And here's a toothbrush and a flannel for both of you,' she said, handing the items over. 'Those are brand new so don't go losing them. You'll need them at the orphanage.'

Just then the kitchen door opened and Mrs Murgatroyd came out. 'Line up for supper,' she called. 'Quietly,' she added, sternly.

Jack and Ella followed the other children in a line into the kitchen, where they were given soup and bread by the two ladies. As they waited to be served, Jack nudged Ella and whispered.

'Look, there's the back door that Tom told us about,' he said.

Ella looked over to the corner of the room, past a big sink and cupboard full of cups and plates. There was a large wooden door and, just as Tom had said, there was a key in the lock.

'Cool,' whispered Ella. 'Let's get out of here as soon as we can.'

After supper the children were made to line up again, this time to clean their teeth in a little bathroom next to the kitchen. Then they all had to change into their night clothes and get into bed.

Mrs Murgatroyd walked up and down the hall making sure everybody was in bed.

'Now listen to me carefully,' she said. 'There is to be *no* talking after lights out. Do I make myself clear?'

'Yes Mrs Murgatroyd,' chanted the children in unison.

'Good,' said Mrs Murgatroyd. 'We have an early start tomorrow. This hall must be vacated by 09.00 hours sharp, as the church requires it for choir practice. We will then walk to the railway station. We will take a local train and then change to the express at Richmond. I will be waking everybody up at 08.00 and anybody who does not get out of bed will get no breakfast. Clear?'

The children chanted again, and Mrs Murgatroyd marched to the door, turned out the lights and drew the curtain across a corner of the church hall where she and Miss Withers had their beds.

As it was still quite early in the evening, there was still some daylight left coming through the curtains of the hall. Jack and Ella could see each other easily through the gloom.

'Ready?' whispered Jack.

'Not yet,' replied Ella. 'Let's wait until it's

completely dark. Then there's no chance anyone can see us.'

'OK,' said Jack. 'But don't fall asleep.'

'I won't,' said Ella. 'I'm too nervous.'

They lay back down in their beds and waited for what seemed like hours, until finally it became very dark in the hall. Then Ella cautiously got out of bed and changed out of her nightclothes, while Jack did the same. All the time they were looking anxiously around to make sure none of the other children woke up, in case they made a noise which might attract Mrs Murgatroyd.

Once they were dressed, they began to tiptoe towards the kitchen door. They stopped short as they heard someone whisper.

'Hey,' came the voice from one of the beds. They saw a tousled head appear from under the covers. It was Tom.

'Good luck,' he whispered, and closed one eye briefly.

'Thanks!' said Jack, wishing that he was able to wink like that as well.

They carefully opened the door into the kitchen. It was pitch black inside.

'I can't see a thing,' whispered Jack.

'Me either,' said Ella. 'Wait, what's that over there?'

Ella pointed to the corner of the room where they could just make out a sliver of moonlight coming from under the back door.

'That must be the door,' said Jack. 'Come on.'

They groped their way to the corner of the room

but suddenly, there was the sound of a dull thud and Ella cried out in pain.

'Ow,' she said. 'I just hit my leg on something,' she said. 'I think it's the plate dresser.' She held her hand out to steady herself and suddenly there was a loud crash as a china cup fell from the shelf on to the floor.

'Quick,' hissed Jack. 'Let's get out of here before the Murder Droid catches us!'

He rushed to the door and turned the handle, but the door was stuck fast. He groped for the key in the lock, but all he could feel was the little flap that covered the keyhole. There was no key in it.

The room lit up in a blaze of light. Jack and Ella turned around, shielding their eyes from the glare.

Standing in the doorway, wearing a hideous purple dressing gown and with her hair in curlers, was Mrs Murgatroyd. She was holding up a key.

'Is this what you were looking for?' she asked angrily.

Jack and Ella said nothing, and looked down at the floor.

'I saw you looking at that back door during supper,' said Mrs Murgatroyd, 'and so I took the precaution of removing the key. I do, however, have another key, and that is for *this* door.' She pointed to the door into the hall.

She took another key from her dressing gown pocket and held it up. 'I have no desire to be chasing young runaways around London in the middle of the night,' she said. 'You will therefore remain in this kitchen until morning.'

'But we don't have any beds, or blankets,' said Ella.

'You should have thought of that before,' said Mrs Murgatroyd. 'Think of our poor troops in France who are sleeping in prison camps tonight. You should be ashamed of yourselves. Now, I do not wish to hear from you again until morning.'

Before Jack and Ella could say anything, Mrs Murgatroyd turned out the light and closed the door behind her. They heard the rattle of the key and realised she had locked them inside the completely dark kitchen.

Chapter Twelve
Danger on a Train

'What do we do now, Jack?' said Ella. 'We can't just stay here in the dark.'

Jack thought for a moment. He could just make out Ella's face in the gloom. 'What about the windows?' he asked. 'Maybe we could climb out?'

'No good,' said Ella with a sigh. 'The windows are really high up in here. I noticed them earlier. There's no way we could climb out.'

'OK,' said Jack. 'I suppose there's nothing we can do. We'll just have to wait until morning.' He sat down on the floor, which felt cold and greasy.

Ella sat down. 'Yuk,' she said. 'This floor is gross, and it's cold. I don't want to stay in here.'

'We might get a chance to get away tomorrow,' said Jack. 'The Murder Droid said we were going on a train somewhere.'

'Maybe,' said Ella, glumly. 'I guess it's our last chance.'

Suddenly there was a clicking noise and a torch flashed round the room. Jack and Ella turned towards the door.

'Shh!' said a voice. 'Don't say anything.' Jack and

Ella blinked in the torchlight and saw a figure come into the kitchen, but they could not make out who it was.

'It's alright,' said a voice. 'It's only me. Miss Withers.'

'We've already been told off by Mrs Murde...I mean, Mrs Murgatroyd,' said Jack.

'Keep your voice down,' said Miss Withers, shutting the door behind her. She placed some sort of bundle on the kitchen table. 'I know, I heard her talking. She's asleep now and I got her key from her dressing gown pocket.'

'Are you going to let us escape?' said Ella.

'Certainly not,' said Miss Withers. 'I've come to give you some blankets so you can sleep on the floor.'

'Oh,' said Jack, in a disappointed voice.

Miss Withers laid out the blankets on the floor and rolled two up to make pillows.

'There,' she said. 'I couldn't bear the thought of you sleeping on the cold floor. Now get into bed.'

Jack and Ella got under the blankets and lay down. Miss Withers then took some bread rolls out of her pocket and placed them on the table.

'Have these as well. Mrs Murgatroyd won't let you have any breakfast tomorrow. But don't let her see them, will you?'

'OK,' said Jack and Ella.

'And make sure you hide the blankets as well before she unlocks the door in the morning. Put them in the broom cupboard over there.' She pointed to a door in the corner of the kitchen.

'Alright, we will,' said Jack.

'Now goodnight, dears,' said Miss Withers. 'Don't think too badly of Mrs Murgatroyd. Her husband was killed early on in the war and she took it rather badly. She isn't a bad sort really.'

Miss Withers clicked off her torch and shut the door. Jack and Ella heard the key turning in the lock. They did their best to settle down on the uncomfortable floor, and before long managed to fall into a fitful sleep.

Ella was woken up by a beam of light hitting her eyes as the sun rose. She felt stiff all over from sleeping on the hard floor. She suddenly remembered where she was, and the events of the previous night, and shook Jack.

'Jack, wake up,' she said. 'We've got to hide these blankets.'

'What time is it?' said Jack sleepily.

'I don't know,' said Ella. Then she noticed an old fashioned clock on the kitchen wall.

'It's nearly eight,' said Ella. 'Quick, the Murder Droid will be in here soon.'

They both jumped up and bundled the blankets into a heap, which they shoved into the broom cupboard in the corner. They then wolfed down the bread rolls that Miss Withers had given them.

Just as they had finished eating, they heard Mrs Murgatroyd calling in the hall.

'Eight o'clock, everybody up. Quickly now, look sharp!'

They heard the key turn in the lock and then Mrs Murgatroyd strode in.

'That includes you two,' she snapped. 'Line up for the ablutions.'

'The what?' said Ella.

Mrs Murgatroyd sighed. 'The bathroom. Fetch your toothbrushes and flannels from your beds.'

Once again Jack and Ella had to queue to use the little bathroom, and then they had to push their beds to the side of the hall. A group of men and boys from the church were already starting to drift in to the hall for choir practice before the morning service.

'You'll need your things,' said Miss Withers, who wrapped Jack and Ella's night clothes into two brown paper parcels and handed them to them.

'Now come along everybody,' ordered Miss Withers. 'We have a train to catch. Form a crocodile.'

'What the heck is she talking about?' asked Ella.

Jack noticed the other children lining up in pairs and holding hands. 'I think she means walk in a line.'

Ella rolled her eyes. 'Does she think we're babies?' she said to Jack.

'Quite the opposite,' came a voice from behind. Ella turned round to see Mrs Murgatroyd standing over her. 'I think you're rather too grown up, young lady, which is why I intend to keep a close eye on you. Now, hold hands with this boy.'

Ella reluctantly took Jack's hand as the children filed out in a long line through the doors of the hall. As they marched to the railway station, Mrs Murgatroyd walked alongside Jack and Ella, keeping watch all the time. They could not even whisper to one another in case she heard.

The streets were quiet, except for a few people

going to early morning church services. A policeman on the beat noticed them and walked in front of them to stop traffic when they crossed the roads. Within five minutes they arrived at a small railway station. Jack noticed it had a rather odd name: 'Gospel Oak.' He couldn't help thinking he'd heard the name before, but he couldn't think where.

Once Miss Withers had bought the tickets, the group filed on to the railway platform and before long, a small steam train came puffing along the line and stopped. A guard began opening doors and the children began to get on the train. It was one of the old-fashioned carriages which had small compartments, and no corridor to allow passengers to walk through the train.

Mrs Murgatroyd was momentarily distracted by some of the other children trying to put money in a machine which gave out chocolate bars. While she was telling them off, Jack whispered to Ella.

'Let's make a run for it,' he said. 'This could be our last chance.'

Ella looked around and sighed. 'No way,' she said. 'Look.' She pointed to the platform exit and saw the policeman who had escorted them to the station was standing there, making sure they all got on the train.

Before they could say anything more, Jack and Ella felt pudgy fingers on their shoulders steering them towards the train.

'Come along you two,' said Mrs Murgatroyd. 'You're sitting with me in this compartment.'

They clambered into the train compartment which had two long seats on either side, with luggage racks above them. The guard slammed the door and with a loud hissing of steam the train set off. Jack noticed that the door into the compartment had a handle on the inside, which turned as the porter closed it. He also noticed a little chain above the door with a sign next to it which stated *'To stop train in emergency pull chain. Penalty for improper use: £5.'*

'Now sit down quietly,' said Mrs Murgatroyd as she plonked her ample behind on to the seat. 'I do not wish to hear any talking.'

Jack and Ella sat next to each other opposite Mrs Murgatroyd.

'You two over here, beside me,' she said. 'Come along now.'

Ella and Jack reluctantly moved over next to Mrs Murgatroyd. The four other children in the compartment settled down quietly to read comics that they had brought with them, or just looked out of the window.

Jack and Ella watched the bomb-damaged, grimy streets of wartime London roll by outside the train, and a few minutes later they pulled into another station. Jack's heart leapt when he saw the name of the station.

'Hampstead Heath,' he exclaimed. 'Ella, this is where we used to live. Our old house is near here.'

'Silence,' snapped Mrs Murgatroyd. 'I said no talking. But I shall inform the authorities at the orphanage of what you said. I will ask them to check the names of all missing children from the Hampstead Heath area. Then perhaps we can get to the bottom of who you two really are.'

Ella glared at Mrs Murgatroyd as she sat back in her seat with a self-satisfied look on her face. Just then, a man wearing a flat cap and a raincoat opened the door from the platform and looked in. He saw that the compartment was full of children. 'Oh, er, sorry,' he said. 'I'll try another compartment.'

As he shut the door Jack noticed again that the little handle on the inside turned at the same time.

With a jerk the train set off and soon they were travelling through a cutting with trees on either side. Mrs Murgatroyd leant forward and snatched a comic out of the hand of one of the little children opposite.

'I won't have you reading these penny dreadfuls,' she said, looking at the comic with disdain. 'You should read a proper book, not trash.'

Ella felt anger boiling up inside her and could hold it in no longer. She leapt up from her seat, quivering with rage.

'That is just totally not OK,' she said loudly. 'You should be happy this girl is reading something even if it's a comic book. Where I come from some kids don't read anything at all.'

Mrs Murgatroyd gazed open-mouthed at Ella. She was momentarily unable to speak.

'You're just totally gross and nasty,' continued Ella. 'You pick on kids and treat them like, like, they were dirt! Someone like you shouldn't be allowed to work with children!'

Mrs Murgatroyd went very red in the face and started blustering. 'I have never...heard...such insolence!'

Ella just stared back and folded her arms. Before

Mrs Murgatroyd continued, the train suddenly stopped with a screech of brakes. The children on the seat facing towards the direction of travel tumbled forwards into a big heap on top of Mrs Murgatroyd. One of the children's cases tumbled off the luggage rack and burst open on the floor; clothes and a teddy bear spilled out. Ella struggled to remain upright. She turned to see Jack by the door standing on the seat. He had just pulled the emergency stop chain.

'Jack!' shouted Ella. 'What the heck's going on?'

'Come on, quick,' said Jack. He jumped off the seat and pushed the door handle down. Just as he had hoped, the door immediately swung open. Jack looked down and gulped; the ground seemed a long way down.

'What are you doing?' screeched Mrs Murgatroyd, who was trying to disentangle herself from the heap of children, clothes and bags on the floor. 'Close that door this instant!'

'Come on Ella,' said Jack. He turned and pulled her towards the door. Then he took a deep breath and jumped out, bending his knees as he landed on the gravel. He felt a thud next to him as Ella jumped out and landed next to him.

They could still hear Mrs Murgatroyd shouting from inside the compartment, and further down the train they saw a man with a black cap lean out of the window.

'Hey, you, get back inside,' he shouted angrily.

'What now?' said Ella.

'Run!' said Jack.

Ella did not need any more encouragement. They

both scrambled along the gravel next to the train until they were in front of it. They continued running along the line, their hearts pounding. Jack sprinted in front but Ella, with her ill-fitting shoes, struggled to keep up. Jack heard a crash and looked round to find Ella sprawled across the railway tracks.

'Get up, quick,' said Jack. 'They're still chasing us!'

'I can't,' gasped Ella. 'My foot's stuck under this rail.'

Jack saw that Ella's foot had become trapped under a rail. He also saw that the man who had shouted at them from the train was now running towards them, with Mrs Murgatroyd not far behind.

'Get off!' shouted the man. 'Get off the tracks! There's a train coming!'

'Jack, help me!' screamed Ella, pulling her leg desperately.

Jack tried to pull Ella's leg out from under the rail but it was stuck fast. He felt the rail shudder and vibrate, and heard a loud, piercing whistle. He turned round to see a train rushing towards them from the opposite direction. There was then a horrible screeching sound as the driver slammed on the brakes. Sparks began to fly from the wheels but the train did not even slow down.

With no time to even think, Jack reached down and deftly unbuckled the little strap on the shoe.

'Pull your foot out,' he said.

Ella quickly pulled her foot out and dived off the tracks. Jack had just enough time to snatch the shoe from under the rail before the train hurtled past. He and Ella threw themselves against the grassy bank by the railway line, as far as possible from the train.

Within seconds the train screeched to a halt a short distance down the line. Jack saw the driver get out and talk to the guard and Mrs Murgatroyd, who by now were only a short distance away.

'Let's get out of here,' said Jack, giving Ella her shoe.

Ella shoved her foot in the shoe and hurriedly buckled it. The two children then continued running along the line.

They could hear Mrs Murgatroyd yelling behind them. 'You won't get far! I shall inform the police!'

Ella and Jack ran into a small wood near the line and just kept on running, past houses and back gardens, until they could no longer hear any shouting. Exhausted, they flung themselves behind some bushes on a sandy bank, and tried to get their breath back.

Jack turned round and peeped through the bushes; in the distance he could just make out the trains next to each other on the track. There was the sound of a whistle and then the two trains began to move off.

'I think we're OK,' said Jack. 'Looks like the train's gone.'

'What if the Murder Droid got off to find us?' said Ella, between breaths.

'I don't think she will,' said Jack. 'She's too fat to run this far anyway.'

'My heart's pounding,' said Ella.

'Mine too,' said Jack. 'We must have run miles!'

'That was totally cool what you did,' said Ella.

'What?' asked Jack. 'Pulling that chain thing?'

'And pulling my leg out of that track too,' said Ella. 'I don't know how you did it.'

'It wasn't much,' shrugged Jack. 'I could see pulling didn't do any good so I thought maybe if I loosened the shoe you could get your foot out.'

'It was *awesome*,' said Ella.

'Well so was you telling off the Murder Droid,' said Jack. 'Did you see her face?'

Ella laughed. 'Yes, she totally didn't believe a kid could yell at her like that. But she deserved it.'

After they had finally got their breath back, the two children sat up and cautiously looked around them. They were now in a deeply wooded area with no buildings or paths to be seen.

'At least we got away,' said Ella. 'Now we can get back to Peter's house and get into the shelter.'

'There's just one small problem,' said Jack, as he looked around at the dense trees and undergrowth.

'What?' asked Ella.

Jack sighed. 'We've got no idea where on earth we are,' he said. 'How are we going to find our way back?'

Chapter Thirteen
Lost in the Woods

'I don't understand,' said Ella. 'How can we be lost?' I thought we were still in London.'

'We are,' said Jack. 'But I think we're on Hampstead Heath. It's really big, with loads of woods and paths and stuff.'

'Can't you remember the way back to the railway line?' said Ella.

'Not really, I was running so fast,' said Jack. 'Anyway we probably shouldn't go back that way. They might be looking for us.'

'But didn't you live around here?' asked Ella. 'When you were in your old house?'

'Yes,' replied Jack. 'But I don't remember any of this area. I always went on walks with mum and dad and they knew the way.'

'OK,' said Ella. 'I guess it must look different because the trees from our time would be much smaller now. All we can do is just walk in one direction and keep walking. We'll have to find out where are soon. After all, we're not in the Navajo Desert.'

The children set off through the trees and

eventually came across a path where they saw a man walking his dog. He passed them by without a second glance.

'What if we ask someone?' said Ella.

'Too risky,' said Jack. 'They might get suspicious and tell someone.'

'OK,' sighed Ella. 'Let's just keep walking.'

It seemed as if they had walked for hours, but still they were surrounded by trees and bushes. Eventually Jack sat down under a tree and Ella followed.

'I'm hungry,' said Ella. 'We haven't had anything since breakfast and it must be lunchtime now.'

'Look,' said Jack, pointing in front of him. 'There's a blackberry bush. We can eat some of those.'

Sure enough, a short distance away was a prickly bramble bush laden with ripe berries. Jack and Ella picked as many as they could and crammed them into their mouths.

'That is sooo good,' said Ella. 'I always thought eating stuff off trees was kind of gross, but these taste great.'

After they had eaten as many berries as they could, Jack peered into the distance.

'Look over there,' he said, pointing.

'What?' asked Ella.

'Can you see some houses? White ones?'

Ella looked closely. 'I think so,' she said.

'I think I know where we are!' said Jack. 'I think that's our old street up there. Come on.'

Jack got up and hurried towards the small patches of white which were just visible through the trees.

Ella followed close behind. A few minutes later, they emerged through a gap in the trees into a little dead-end road with some old white-painted houses on it.

'I don't believe it,' said Jack. 'This is my old road. And that's our old house!'

'You're right,' said Ella. 'I remember it now from when I came last time. "Heath View", that was the name of your house, wasn't it? Look, it's that one.'

Sure enough, the house at the end of the road had a small painted sign on the gate with that very name upon it.

Jack spent a few moments gazing at the house. 'It doesn't really look much different,' he said. 'But there's no garage, and all the flowers and stuff in the garden are different.'

'I guess they would be,' said Ella. 'After all, a garden must grow a lot of different stuff over 80 years.'

'I suppose,' said Jack. 'Hey, do you think we could ask to look around?'

'Don't be stupid,' said Ella, rolling her eyes. 'What are we going to say to the owners? "oh hi there, we're from the future, could we look around?"'

'I suppose not,' said Jack. 'It would be cool to see my bedroom though.'

'We can't risk it,' said Ella. She noticed a curtain twitching behind one of the windows in the house. 'We're already attracting too much attention. Come on, let's keep going. We could be walking a long time.'

'Wait,' said Jack. 'I know where we are now. I

remember the way to the tube station. We could get to Peter's house on the tube!'

'Are you sure?' asked Ella. 'How do you know they have a subway, I mean a tube, in this time?'

'I'm pretty sure they had the tube in 1940,' said Jack. 'I remember in school reading about people sleeping in there during the bombing raids.'

'Well let's try,' said Ella. 'But we don't have any money for tickets,' she added.

Jack nodded and thought for a moment. 'We'll cross that bridge when we come to it,' said Jack. 'That's what dad always says.'

Jack and Ella began walking along the lane. After a few minutes Jack was pleased to see that the street was not much different from his own time, and eventually it led onto a main road lined with shops, which did not seem to have changed much either, except that there were fewer cars and the shops had long queues of women outside them, waiting with shopping baskets to buy food.

At the end of the road Jack saw a familiar red-tiled building with the blue and white London Underground sign.

'It's the station!' he said. 'I knew it would still be here.'

They approached the building and Jack pointed to the map of the underground network which was fixed to the wall of the station. It looked much the same as how he remembered it.

'I knew I was right,' he said proudly. 'Look, we can get back to Peter's house easily. It's just a few stops along the line.' He traced his finger along the map until it arrived at Northgate Park station.

'Come on, let's get the train,' said Jack.

'Aren't you forgetting something?' asked Ella. 'How do we get a ticket? We don't have any cards or money.'

Jack grinned. 'Cross that bridge when we come to it,' he said. 'I've got an idea.'

The two children walked nonchalantly into the station. Jack was pleased to see that the station was not much different to how he remembered it. There was a little window where you could buy tickets, and a lift which went down to the platform. Next to the lift was a staircase.

'See that ticket window,' whispered Jack. 'All we need to do is walk past that and duck down, and they won't see us.'

'Isn't that kind of risky?' said Ella. 'What if we get caught?'

'Well we won't be in any worse trouble than we already are,' said Jack.

'I guess,' said Ella. 'It seems wrong to get on the train without paying, but there's no way we can get any money.'

'It's an emergency,' said Jack. 'Come on.'

The station was quiet, it being Sunday afternoon, and there were no other people there to see them. They walked around the edge of the wall, and when they came close to the ticket window, they both crouched down and edged past the window ledge. Once they had got past, they stood up and Jack turned towards the lift.

He froze in horror as he saw a uniformed guard by

the lift doors watching them.

'What do you think you're playing at?' said the guard. He was an oldish man and had a mean look about him, with a short cigarette stub in his mouth.

'Quick,' said Jack. 'The stairs!'

He grabbed Ella's hand and pulled her towards the spiral staircase. Their feet clanged on the metal steps as they ran downward.

'You come back here!' shouted the guard. 'I'll report this!'

Jack and Ella became dizzy as they ran round and round at breakneck speed. The staircase seemed to go down forever, and they could hear far away the sound of the guard's feet on the steps as he chased after them.

Finally they reached the platform, just as a train was pulling in. Jack had no idea if it was the right one, but decided in a split second to get on. He dragged Ella on board and they both crouched down behind some seats. Just then they saw the guard emerge from the staircase, but it was too late – the doors of the train slid shut and it pulled away. They caught a last glimpse through the window of the guard shaking his fist at them from the staircase.

'I'm exhausted,' said Ella, as she plonked herself down into a seat. 'We've been running and walking all day.'

'Same here,' said Jack. 'We can rest for a bit now though.' He looked around the carriage to make sure there was nobody listening. There wasn't anyone else around except for two soldiers at the far end of the carriage, who appeared to be asleep. 'Good idea to sneak under the window though, wasn't it? Otherwise we might have been walking all day.'

'Well it was good until that guy nearly caught us,' said Ella. She looked down at her feet. 'I thought for a minute I was going to trip on these stupid shoes again.' She slumped back in her seat and then sprang forward with a look of concern on her face.

'Hey, we are on the right train, aren't we?' she said. 'I mean, we didn't even check.'

Jack looked at the map of the line above the window. 'If the next station is East Hampstead, then we're OK,' he said.

Sure enough, that was the next station, and so the children relaxed for the rest of the journey, and read the old-fashioned advertisements on the carriage walls, for things they'd never heard of like Oxo Cubes and Euthymol toothpaste. A few more people got on at different stations, but nobody paid them any attention. After about fifteen minutes the train emerged from the tunnel into bright sunshine and slowed until it stopped at a station.

'This is it,' said Jack. 'Northgate Park. It doesn't look much different from how it does in our own time.'

Ella and Jack got off the train and began to walk along the platform towards the exit. Ella stopped and held Jack back.

'Wait,' she said, pointing at the exit gate. There was a guard standing by the gate, collecting tickets from passengers as they filed through the narrow gate.

'How are we going to get past that guy?' said Ella.

'There must be another way out,' said Jack, looking

around. All he could see was a high fence running along the side of the platform. There was no way they could climb over.

'Oh no,' said Ella. 'He's coming towards us.'

Jack felt his heart sink. They had come all this way and now were about to be caught again.

'What are you two waiting for?' said the man. 'Come along, tickets please.'

A thought struck Jack and he smiled at the man.

'Sorry,' he said. 'We're supposed to get off at Northgate Central, not Northgate Park. Can we get the next train?'

'Alright then,' said the man. 'Happens sometimes. Just get the next train. Should be here in a couple of minutes.'

Then the man checked his watch and turned away from them. He then unlocked a little door in the station building and walked inside.

'Quick,' whispered Jack. 'Now's our chance, while he's not looking.'

'Don't run,' said Ella. 'It might attract attention, and I don't want to fall over again in these stupid old-lady shoes.'

They walked briskly past the gate and out into the street by the park. It all looked much the same as Jack remembered it, except this time much of the grass in the park had gone. In its place were rows and rows of plants and vegetables. A few old men were tending to the plants and watering them.

'They must be growing food,' said Jack. 'Remember what Peter said, about rationing? There isn't enough food in the shops so people have to grow it themselves.'

'I'm really hungry,' said Ella, who was eyeing a pile of carrots stacked by the pathway. 'Do you think we could take something?'

'Better not,' said Jack. 'It's not ours and anyway, we don't want to get noticed.'

'OK,' sighed Ella. 'How are we going to find Peter's house?'

'That's the easy part,' said Jack. 'Dad told me if I ever get lost just follow the railway line, because that goes past our house.'

The two children kept as close as they could to the railway line and walked through the quiet Sunday afternoon streets until they reached Cotswold Gardens.

'What do we do now?' said Ella. 'We don't want anyone to see us getting into the shelter.'

'We don't have much choice,' said Jack. 'It won't be dark for ages so we can't wait until night-time. Let's just keep our heads down and get in the shelter as quick as we can.'

They walked along the street as nonchalantly as they could, with their heads bowed so that nobody could see their faces. They didn't even look at the smouldering remains of the house that had been bombed as they passed by. Nobody seemed to be around, so when they reached Peter's house they quickly changed direction and walked briskly down the side passage. When they got to the gate, Jack peeked through a hole in the wood.

'The coast's clear,' he said. 'Come on.'

Jack opened the gate as quietly as he could, and he

and Ella sidled along the fence until they reached the little hedge at the bottom of the garden. After a final glance at the house to make sure nobody was around, Jack led the way into the shelter. He then stepped back. There was somebody inside.

'Can't get rid of you two, can I?' said a cheerful voice in the gloom.

'Peter!' said Jack and Ella at the same time, both with relief in their voices.

'What happened to you? I thought the police must have caught you. Mother was terribly cross about it all. She thinks I've got into bad company.'

'With who?' asked Ella.

'You two of course,' said Peter. 'She's still angry with me so that's why I'm lying low in here most of the time. But never mind that. What happened to you?'

With excited voices Jack and Ella described how they had been caught by the police and then handed over to Mrs Murgatroyd, and how they had escaped from the train and made their way back.

'I say,' said Peter. 'that's almost as good as an adventure story. But what are you going to do now?'

'Remember we said the shelter travels through time when a bomb goes off?' said Ella.

'Oh yes,' said Peter. 'And the next big raid is going to be tomorrow. You found it out using a computer.'

'Right,' said Jack. 'So we need to make sure we're in here tomorrow when the raid happens.'

'You can stay in here tonight,' said Peter. 'There's blankets and I'll bring some food later when it's dark. Mother won't find out, as long as you keep quiet.'

'What about our clothes?' said Jack. 'We'd better give you these old ones back. We won't need them in our own time.'

Peter agreed and once again the boys stood outside the shelter while Ella changed, then Ella came out and Jack got changed. Once they were back in the shelter, Peter looked at them.

'I say, you do look a bit odd in those togs,' he said. 'I should have taken a picture of you dressed like that, but I've run out of film.'

Peter then noticed the newspaper that Jack had brought with him from the future. It had been left on the lower bunk. 'Do you think I could keep this?' he asked. 'Sort of proof that all this actually happened?'

'If you like,' said Jack. 'But probably best not to show anyone or they might start asking awkward questions.'

'Good point,' said Peter. 'I'll keep it safely hidden in the suitcase under my bed.'

'There's just one problem about staying the night here,' said Ella. 'What happens when one of us needs the bathroom?'

'That's not a problem,' laughed Peter. 'Just go in the bushes.' He pointed to the corner of the garden.

'Ew,' said Ella, with a look of disgust on her face.

'Doesn't bother me,' said Jack, with a shrug.

'That's because boys are mostly gross,' said Ella.
Ella and Jack settled down in the shelter and when it was dark, Peter sneaked out with some food from the kitchen for their supper, and then crept back into the house. Since both children were very tired from the long day, they soon fell asleep on the bunk beds.

Ella woke first, as the early morning light streamed through the doorway of the shelter. She had an urgent need to visit the bathroom, as unlike Jack, she had refused to follow Peter's suggestion about using the bushes.

The house looked completely quiet, and all the curtains were drawn. She thought for a moment, then decided to risk it. She crept across the lawn to the kitchen door and turned the handle. It was unlocked. She remembered having seen a little downstairs bathroom next to the kitchen when she had been talking to PC Henderson by the door. Sure enough, there it was, and so she crept across the kitchen and went in.

After she had finished, she decided against flushing in case it attracted attention. Instead she eased open the door as quietly as possible.

She looked up and realised there was no way out. Standing in the middle of the kitchen, wearing a dressing gown and with a horrified expression on her face, was Peter's mother.

Chapter Fourteen
Caught Again

After what seemed like ages, Mrs Bennett finally spoke. 'Just what on earth do you think you are doing here?' she asked. 'I thought I'd seen the last of you when we had the police here. How did you get in here?'

'I…I'm sorry,' said Ella. 'I was just using your bathroom. The door was unlocked.'

'I can't see how it can have been, as I always keep it locked. I told Peter never to have anything to do with you again, so what are you doing here?'

'Peter doesn't know about me coming in here,' said Ella. It was sort of true, anyway, she thought to herself.

Just then Peter walked in to the kitchen. 'Who are you talking to, mother?' he asked, and then stopped short when he saw Ella. 'Oh crumbs,' he said.

'I told you never to speak to those children, Peter,' said Mrs Bennett. 'So what is this girl doing in our kitchen?'

'I'm just trying to help Ella and Jack, mother,' said Peter. 'They've got nowhere else to stay so I let them sleep in the shelter.'

Mrs Bennett noticed half a loaf of bread on the worktop. 'And been feeding them as well on our rations, I suppose?' she said, angrily. 'There was nearly a whole loaf there last night. I suppose you crept out and gave something to them and left the door unlocked.'

'I...we couldn't let them starve,' said Peter.

Mrs Bennett was on the verge of tears. 'After all we've been through...if your father was here this wouldn't have happened. Causing trouble and bringing the police round, in front of all the neighbours. Well I'm not standing for it. Where's the other one, the boy?'

'Here,' said a voice. They all turned and saw Jack had walked into the kitchen. 'I heard all the talking from the garden and I came to explain. It's not Peter's fault, he was just helping us because we've got nowhere to go. Sorry to have caused you any trouble. We'll go now. Come on Ella.'

'Oh no you don't,' said Mrs Bennett. She stood between Jack and the kitchen door. 'You've already run away from the police once. I'm not having this happening again.'

She shut the kitchen door and turned the key in the lock, then strode over to the other door which led into the hallway.

'Where are you going, mother?' said Peter.

'To telephone the police,' said Mrs Bennett. 'You're to stay in here until they arrive.'

'But...' began Peter.

'No buts,' said Mrs Bennett. 'I'm not having children running wild just because there's a war on

149

and their fathers are away. It's about time you learnt some discipline. I'm locking this door and don't bother trying to get out through the window because that's locked too.' She turned on her heel and slammed the kitchen door behind her. The children heard the key turn in the lock and then Mrs Bennett's voice from the hallway as she picked up the telephone. 'Police please,' she said.

'Well that's torn it,' said Peter. 'I suppose you came in to use the lavatory.'

Ella nodded. 'Oh well,' said Peter. 'Can't be helped now.'

'But we can't just sit here,' said Jack. 'We've got to stay in the shelter for when the air raid starts. If the police turn up they'll take us away and we'll never be able to get back to our own time.'

'What if we break the window?' said Ella, in an excited voice.

'Don't be daft,' said Peter. 'Mother will hear and she'll chase after us until she gets us and we'll be in even more trouble.'

The children sat in sullen silence until about twenty minutes later, they heard a car pull up outside. There was a knock at the door and they heard Mrs Bennett talking to somebody.

The kitchen door was unlocked and Mrs Bennett walked in. Behind her was a tall man in police uniform. It was PC Henderson.

'They're in here,' said Mrs Bennett. 'I expect you'll want to take them to the police station straight away.'

'I'd like a bit of chat with them first, if you don't

mind, madam, ' said PC Henderson. 'I think a cup of tea might do us all good as well.'

'Oh…well alright then, I suppose,' said Mrs Bennett. She went to the sink and began making some tea.

PC Henderson unbuckled his helmet and placed it on the kitchen table. 'Hot in those blooming things,' he said, mopping his brow with a handkerchief.

Ella spoke first. 'We're really sorry, officer, but…'

'Just a minute,' said PC Henderson, raising his hand. 'I'm not particularly interested in what you've got to say. I've had that Mrs Murgatroyd on the telephone to me several times since yesterday. She says you jumped off a train and nearly got yourselves killed.'

'We didn't have any choice,' said Jack urgently. 'We keep trying to tell you we've got to get back…'

'Back to the future in a flying Anderson shelter, yes, you've said that before, young man,' said PC Henderson. 'Well you're going to have to change your tune because you're in very serious trouble now. Mrs Murgatroyd wants to have you both put in an Approved School.'

'What…what's an approved school?' asked Ella.

PC Henderson sighed. 'It's another name for a prison for children,' he said. 'The authorities have got enough on their plates with the war, and they don't want youngsters running around causing trouble. Mrs Murgatroyd wants to set an example.'

'Will I have to go to prison as well?' asked Peter. Mrs Bennett inhaled sharply and dropped a cup on the counter as she made the tea.

'Nobody's going to prison,' said PC Henderson. 'Not if I can help it. Certainly not you, Peter. You come from a good home and that's the best place for you. But you two – Jack and Ella – well I've got other plans for you.'

'What plans?' asked Jack nervously.

Mrs Bennett brought over a pot of tea and poured a cup for PC Henderson and herself.

'Aren't the kiddies getting any?' he asked.

'Oh, yes alright then,' said Mrs Bennett. She poured cups of tea for the three children.

PC Henderson swallowed a mouthful of tea. 'Ah, that's better,' he said. 'Now about you two. Do you know what a foster home is?'

Jack and Ella both shook their heads.

'Well,' said PC Henderson, 'it's sort of a family for children who don't have any parents. It's not like an orphanage or a prison or anything like that. It's a loving home. Now, my sister Alice runs a place like that down in Devon on the coast. It's a lovely big house near the beach, and I'm sure she'd have you if I asked. What do you say?'

'It sounds real nice,' said Ella, trying to sound convincing. 'But we'd really just like to stay here.'

'I don't think so, young lady,' said Mrs Bennett. 'I'm struggling enough to feed Peter.'

'Look,' said PC Henderson. 'I've seen this once or twice before. Children who've run away from home. Even kids whose parents have been killed in an air raid. They wouldn't tell anyone what happened. That's fine by me.'

'But we didn't run away from home and our

parents are alive,' protested Jack. 'Well…I mean, they haven't actually been born yet, but they're not dead.'

'This is just what I mean, son,' said PC Henderson gently. 'You keep saying things like this. There's something called shell shock – I saw some of that in the last war. People who've been in too many bomb attacks start talking nonsense and coming out with all sorts of silly ideas. I'm not saying that's what's happened to you, but if you go on like this you'll get sent to a special hospital.'

'You mean a nut house,' said Ella.

'Call it what you want,' said PC Henderson. 'But my advice is you take the offer to stay with my sister. You'll have a nice time there and if you decide you want to tell the truth about where you come from, we'll listen. Now, I'm going to drive you to the police station and once we're there I want you to decide whether I telephone my sister Alice – or Mrs Murgatroyd.'

Jack and Ella looked at each other. They both realised they had no choice but to go along with PC Henderson and that they would never be able to get back home to their own time.

PC Henderson stood up and put his helmet on, then drained the last of his tea from his cup.

'Come along then,' he said, as Jack and Ella stood up. 'Thanks for the tea Mrs Bennett. We'll…'

He was interrupted by a loud wailing noise which seemed to come from everywhere at once.

'Crikey!' exclaimed Peter. 'It's the air-raid sirens. You were right, Jack – there's going to be a raid.'

'Yes!' shouted Jack and Ella, high-fiving each other.

'Don't sound so blooming happy about it,' said PC Henderson. 'It's not going to make any difference. We'll sit it out here and then I'll take you in to the station.'

'Come on Peter,' said Mrs Bennett urgently. 'Get into the Morrison shelter.' She bundled Peter through the door into the dining room.

'You two come along with me,' said PC Henderson. He took firm hold of Jack and Ella's shoulders and steered them through the door behind Peter.

Once they were in the dining room they saw what looked like a large steel table with very thick steel legs, and a wire frame around the edge. Inside was a bed with pillows on it. Mrs Bennett crawled inside and Peter got in next to her. A buzzing, droning sound filled the air and seemed to get louder and louder by the second.

'You get in there,' said PC Henderson. He pushed them towards the table shelter.

'No way!' said Ella. 'We've got to go in the other shelter. The one in the back yard.'

Just then there was a loud series of bangs; like the ones they had heard in the previous air raid. It sounded like a row of huge metal doors being slammed shut. Mrs Bennett screamed and hugged Peter close to her.

'That's the guns at RAF Stanmore opening up,' said PC Henderson. 'The planes will be over any minute. Get in now,' he said, pushing Jack and Ella forward.

Jack and Ella felt their ears pop and a moment later there was a huge crash as a bomb exploded in the next street. The glass doors of the dining room, which led onto the garden, shattered inwards. PC Henderson was knocked to the ground by the blast but Jack and Ella, being much shorter, managed to stay upright.

'Quick,' said Jack. 'Let's get into the shelter.'

The two children scrambled through the broken doorway. They heard a shout from behind and turned. Peter was waving from the table shelter, while his mother buried her face in the pillow.

'Goodbye, and good luck!' he called.

Jack and Ella waved back and ducked out of the room into the garden. They stopped and looked up, open mouthed, as three bomber planes came into view from over the railway line, buzzing like huge black wasps.

'Run for it,' shouted Jack, and began to sprint across the lawn. He dived into the shelter and turned to see Ella standing halfway across the lawn. She seemed to be frozen to the spot with fear.

'Come *on*!' urged Jack.

The air was now full of smoke and he could barely hear anything because of the noise of explosions all around him. Then to his horror, he saw PC Henderson stagger out of the house. Blood was trickling from his forehead where a piece of flying glass had hit him.

'Get back inside,' he shouted, running towards Ella. He scooped her up in his arms and turned back to the house, then hesitated and started to run towards the shelter instead. Jack realised why as the garden was plunged into darkness by the shadow of a bomber plane flying low over the house. It rose up behind PC Henderson and Ella like some terrifying giant bird.

There was a rattling, smashing sound as the plane's machine guns fired across the garden, shattering the greenhouse. PC Henderson sprinted towards the shelter and shoved Ella through the doorway. The garden then disappeared from view as PC Henderson's body blocked the doorway. Then there was another huge explosion. The last thing Jack saw was the inside of the shelter's metal wall crumpling inwards as if a giant's fist had punched through cardboard.

Chapter Fifteen
The Man Next Door

The first thing Jack noticed when he woke up was silence. The noise of guns and bombs had stopped and all he could hear were birds twittering and an electric lawnmower somewhere in the distance.

'Jack, are you OK?' said Ella. She was kneeling over him and shaking him.

'I think so,' said Jack as he sat up and rubbed his head. 'Hey,' he continued. 'Did it work? Are we back in our own time?'

Ella looked around and saw that the shelter had regained its old rusty, dusty look. She peeked out through the doorway and saw that the garden had gone back to looking like a jungle.

'I think so,' said Ella, cautiously. 'Come on, let's get out of here.'

The two children dashed out of the shelter and found the hole in the fence. Just before they climbed through, they heard a voice behind them.

'Hey, come back.'

Jack and Ella looked round and they both gasped. A boy about eleven years old wearing shorts, a white shirt with the sleeves rolled up, and old fashioned glasses was looking at them from behind a clump of weeds.

'Peter?' exclaimed Ella.

The boy blinked then ran off through the undergrowth towards the house. Jack and Ella turned and jumped through the fence and Jack secured the planks in place behind them.

'What's going on?' said Jack, looking at Ella. 'Are we really back?'

Jack tried to look through the small holes in the fence but could see nothing.

'Jack, I'm scared,' said Ella. 'What if we're not back in our own time?'

'Even if we are, who was that boy?' said Jack. 'A ghost?'

'First things first,' said Ella. 'Let's find out what the date is.'

Jack looked towards his house and nodded. 'It all looks much the same as when we left, on Monday morning. I can't wait to tell mum and dad about all this.'

'Wait,' said Ella. 'I don't think we should just yet. They'll just think we made it all up.'

She took her phone out of her hoodie pocket and tried to turn it on, but nothing happened.

'Remember I took that video of Peter on the lawn. Once I charge up this phone, we can prove we really did go back to 1940.'

'OK,' said Jack. 'We'll keep quiet until then. Let's go inside and make sure mum and dad haven't called the police or something to find out where we've been.'

'Good point,' said Ella. 'We left at 9.30 in the morning. So the first thing we need to check is the time and then the date.'

Jack and Ella tried to look innocent as they walked into the kitchen. Mrs Thomas was doing some washing up at the sink.

'Er...hi mum,' said Jack. 'Everything alright?'

Mrs Thomas looked up with a puzzled expression.

'Yes thank you. Why shouldn't it be?'

Jack looked at the clock on the wall and saw that it showed just after 9.30.

'Er...what day is it today, mum?' said Jack.

'Really,' said Mrs Thomas. 'You're not a baby. Look at the calendar on the fridge. It's Monday the 17th of August.'

Ella punched the air. 'Awesome,' she said. 'You haven't missed us, have you Aunt Claire?'

'Missed you?' asked Mrs Thomas. 'Why on earth should I? You've only been out in the garden five minutes.'

'OK mum, thanks, see you later!' shouted Jack. He and Ella dashed out of the kitchen and scrambled up the stairs into Jack's room.

'We're in the clear!' said Jack. 'Nobody noticed we've been away because we came back just a few minutes after we left.'

'I told you that would probably happen,' said Ella. 'Now, let me charge up my phone and we can watch the video from 1940.'

Ella and Jack spent the next few minutes excitedly waiting for the phone to charge. Eventually there was enough power and the screen came on. Ella's fingers swiped up and down the screen but after a few minutes she angrily stabbed her finger repeatedly onto the screen.

'I don't believe it,' she said 'The video's gone.'

'What do you mean, gone?' asked Jack.

'Just disappeared,' said Ella. 'And my other ones too, that I took from the London Eye.'

'Maybe...I don't know, maybe travelling through time damaged the phone or something. Remember the video you took of the London Eye didn't work when we went back to 1940 either.'

Ella slumped down on Jack's bed. 'I guess that's what it must have been. So now we've got nothing to prove we went back.'

'Well...maybe it wouldn't prove anything. The grown ups might say we just faked it or something.'

'I guess,' said Ella. Then after a pause, her face lit up. 'Hey,' she exclaimed. 'What if we went back again, and this time...'

'No way!' interrupted Jack. 'I'm not risking it again. We nearly didn't get back at all. I've seen enough of the old days to last me a lifetime.'

Jack sighed and walked over to the window. He looked out at the creepy old house next door with its jungle garden. Just then, the old door at the back of the house opened with a large creak. Jack saw a man with grey hair lean out and look into the garden.

'Ella!' hissed Jack. 'Look at this!'

Ella stood beside Jack and they both peered out round the side of the curtain so that they could not be seen.

The man called out. 'Peter, come on, give me a hand in here.'

From out of the undergrowth came the boy they had seen before. He followed the man into the house and the door shut behind them.

'Jack, what the heck is going on?' said Ella.

'I don't know,' said Jack. 'Maybe there really are ghosts next door. Maybe we should tell mum.'

'Tell her what?' asked Ella sarcastically. 'That we saw a boy next door that we met last time in 1940, and we think he might be a ghost?'

'You're right,' said Jack. 'I suppose we can't really say anything. I'm keeping close watch on that house though.'

'Jack, I've just thought of something,' said Ella.

'What?' asked Jack.

'What do you think happened to that police guy, Officer Henderson? Was he OK?'

'I don't know,' said Jack. 'He was right outside the shelter when the bomb went off. I don't suppose we'll ever know.'

'That's kind of sad,' said Ella. 'He pretty much saved my life.'

Jack and Ella spent the rest of the day working on the flowerbeds in the garden, but they didn't see or hear anything else happening next door.

Evening came and Mr Thomas arrived home from work. He and Mrs Thomas were relaxing in the garden on deck chairs while Jack and Ella were putting away the garden tools.

There was a knock at the side gate and a grey-haired man looked over it.

'Yes?' said Mr Thomas, half-rising from his deckchair.

'Sorry for the intrusion,' said the man. 'I'm your new neighbour.'

Mr Thomas stood up and walked to the gate. 'From number 39, you mean?' he asked, pointing to the creepy old house.

'Yes, that's right,' said the man. 'Thought I'd say hello. My name's Ralph Bennett.'

'How do you do?' said Mr Thomas. 'I'm James Thomas.' He shook hands with Mr Bennett over the gate. 'Won't you come in?' he asked.

'Oh, thanks very much,' said Mr Bennett. He opened the door and stepped through. With him was the boy that Jack and Ella had seen earlier in the garden.

'This is my son, Peter,' said Mr Bennett.

'Hello Peter,' said Mr Thomas. 'This is my wife Claire,' he said, pointing to Mrs Thomas, who smiled and waved from her deckchair. Mr Thomas looked around.

'And this is my son Jack, and his cousin Ella. She's over from the states on holiday. Kids, come over and say hello.'

Jack and Ella looked at each other with confused expression but walked over and said hello. Peter did not say anything.

'I thought that old place had been abandoned,' said Mr Thomas.

'It had been, sort of,' said Mr Bennett. 'It was my father's place. You might have heard of him actually – Peter Bennett. He was quite a well known

162

photographer and illustrator at one time. My son's named after him.'

'That rings a bell,' said Mrs Thomas. 'Didn't he do those books on nature photography?'

Mr Bennet smiled 'That's right. He died a couple of years ago and it took us a while to sort things out from his will. Now the idea is to do the place up and move in ourselves. My wife's at work at the moment but I've taken a few days off to sort things out here.'

'Have...have you been in there long?' asked Jack, trying to sound as calm as he could.

'I've been coming and going a few times in the evenings after work,' said Mr Bennett. 'There's an awful lot to sort out. The electricity was cut off so I had to look around by torchlight once or twice.'

'Come in and have a drink,' said Mr Thomas.

'Very kind of you, but we should crack on,' said Mr Bennett. 'I've got a load of things to take to the dump and the charity shops before they close. Tell you what, if you like you can have a look around. Take anything you want. It's quite a time capsule in that house.'

'That sounds interesting,' said Mrs Thomas. 'I'm an illustrator myself. I don't suppose there are any drawing materials?'

'Oh, tons,' said Mr Bennett. 'You're welcome to them. I've no use for them, I'm a chartered accountant. And Peter's more interested in computer games than anything in real life, aren't you?'

Peter just shrugged. 'Come on then,' said Mr Bennett. 'Come and have a look round and see what you'd like.'

Everybody walked round through the side passage and across the front garden of the creepy old house.

The grown ups went ahead and Jack, Ella and Peter trailed behind.

'I saw you in the garden before,' said Peter.

'You won't tell anyone we sneaked in, will you?' said Jack.

'Course not,' said Peter. 'Having a secret hole in the fence like that is cool. We can go in and out of each other's gardens. If you want to be friends, I mean.'

'OK,' said Jack.

'I'm only here for a few more days before I go back to the states,' said Ella, 'but I guess we can all hang out.'

'Sounds good,' said Peter, as they approached the front door of the old house. 'But how did you know my name?'

'Er...your dad told us,' said Jack.

'No, I mean before that. When I saw you in the garden.'

Jack felt Ella nudge him in the ribs and decided he shouldn't say anything about travelling back in time. At least not yet.

'Oh, you remind me of someone I used to know called Peter who lived around here,' said Jack. 'He looked a lot like you and I thought it was him.'

Peter seemed satisfied with the explanation. The children caught up with the grown-ups, and Mr Bennett opened the door and they went in to the house.

Jack and Ella noticed that the place hadn't changed

much from what they remembered in 1940, but everything was now very old and dusty. Things were piled up in boxes all over the place, and the boxes had things like 'charity shop' and 'rubbish' written on them in felt pen.

'Excuse the mess,' said Mr Bennett. 'Dad was a bit of a hoarder and in his later years he couldn't manage the place. We tried to help but he was a very independent man.'

'Here are the drawing things, dad,' said Peter, pulling out a box from the dining room.

'Have a look through, why don't you?' said Mr Bennett. 'And kids, there's some photos here of the house years ago. I'm only keeping a few ones of the family. There's lots of pictures in there of people I can't identify. Some of them show your house and this street as well. Quite interesting to see how it's all changed.'

Mrs Thomas began looking through the pens and paper while Jack, Ella and Peter looked at a pile of photos in an old cardboard box. Mr Thomas and Mr Bennett started chatting.

'So you're moving in soon then?' asked Mr Thomas.

'That's right,' replied Mr Bennett. 'Once we've cleared out the place and redecorated. I'd like to refurbish it, it hasn't changed a bit since I was a boy'.

'The house has been in the family a long time?' asked Mr Thomas.

'Oh yes. My grandfather bought it before the war when it was new. Dad lived here nearly all his life. I grew up here but moved away about 30 years ago.'

'Quite a lot of work to do in the garden,' said Mr Thomas, looking out of the window.

'Ah, the jungle, we used to call it,' said Mr Bennett. 'It's always been quite overgrown as long as I can remember, especially at the bottom,' he continued. 'There's even an old wartime bomb shelter down there, I think.'

Jack and Ella looked at each other and pretended to be rummaging through the photos, while they listened carefully to what was being said.

'I was never allowed to play there, though,' said Mr Bennett. 'My father seemed to think it was dangerous. He just let it all get overgrown. I think the real reason was that it got hit during an air raid.'

'Really?' said Mr Thomas. 'Did you hear that, kids? This house was bombed in the war.'

'Not bombed, exactly,' said Mr Bennett. 'It's a bit of a family legend, that's been exaggerated I think. My grandmother was here at the time and she said a bomb dropped on the railway line. A bit of debris hit the shelter and injured a policeman.'

Jack nudged Ella and whispered. 'That must have been when the side of the shelter got all smashed in.'

'What was that?' asked Mr Bennett.

Ella thought quickly. 'Oh, we were just wondering, what happened to the policeman?'

'Hmm, let me think,' said Mr Bennett. 'I remember now. Granny said he ran into the garden to help some local children who were caught out in the air raid. He managed to get them safely in the shelter, but got knocked unconscious by the blast. Granny found him in the garden afterwards and had to call for an ambulance. I think he recovered though.'

'Wow,' said Peter. 'Grandpa never said anything about that when he was alive.'

'I think he didn't really want to as he was probably rather upset about it,' said Mr Bennett.

'What happened to the children ?' asked Jack, with a knowing glance to Ella.

'That was the odd thing,' said Mr Bennett. 'Nobody ever saw them again, according to my grandmother. They were some sort of orphans, I think, and nobody knew who their parents were. I suppose they just ran off.'

'These are some lovely old pens and inks,' said Mrs Thomas. 'Would it be alright if I took them?'

'Of course,' said Mr Bennett. 'And you, kids, have you found any interesting photos?'

Jack and Ella looked up from the box. 'Not really,' said Jack. 'There's only one or two that show a tiny bit of our house in the background.'

'That's a shame,' said Mr Bennett.

'Wow!' said Peter. 'Look at this one! It's a picture of you two.' He held up an old, faded photograph of two children standing in front of an air raid shelter on a sunny day.

'A picture of you two who?' asked Mr Bennett.

'Jack and Ella,' said Peter.

'Don't be silly,' replied Mr Bennett. 'How could there be a picture of Jack and Ella in that box? Let me see.'

Jack and Ella looked at each other in horror. It was the photograph that Peter – the old Peter – had taken of them. Was their secret of travelling back in time about to be discovered?

'Hmm,' said Mr Bennett, peering at the photo. 'I see what you mean. It does look a bit like you two.'

He turned towards Mr Thomas. 'Here, have a look at this. Couple of kids in front of an air raid shelter. Looks like these two had doubles back in the war!'

Jack and Ella sighed with relief as Mr and Mrs Thomas looked at the photo and did not seem suspicious at all. In fact they both chuckled.

'They do look awfully like you,' said Mrs Thomas. 'What a coincidence.'

'Erm, could we keep that one please?' asked Ella.

'Of course,' said Mr Bennett. 'I've no idea who they are, probably friends of dad's, but if you'd like it, be my guest.'

'I never knew there was an air raid shelter in the garden,' said Peter. 'Can we go and look at it?'

'No chance,' said Mr Bennett. 'I tried to get through the other day but it's impenetrable jungle I'm afraid. A child might get through but it could be dangerous. There's broken glass there.'

'Aw,' said Peter. 'I wanted to see it. It would be cool to have a secret shelter.'

'Sorry old chap,' said Mr Bennett. 'The landscape gardeners are coming tomorrow to flatten the garden. You might get to see a few bits of old metal when they clear up. I'm afraid the secrets of the shelter are going to be lost for all time.'

Epilogue
The Mysterious Newspaper

A few days later, Ella was packing, because she was due to go home to New York. Jack was in her room looking at the old picture of them taken in 1940.

'This is all we've got to remind us that it really happened,' said Jack.

'True,' said Ella. 'Give me that a minute.'

Jack handed over the photo and Ella carefully took a picture of it with her phone. 'There,' she said. 'Now we've both got a copy.'

'And now the shelter's gone,' said Jack. 'Look,' he said, pointing out of the window to next door's garden. It was just possible to see the sunken patch of ground where the shelter had been. Workmen were hacking away at all the weeds around it, and putting bits of rotten wood onto a bonfire.

'Come on you two,' called Mrs Thomas up the stairs. 'We've got to get to the airport for Ella's plane.'

Jack helped Ella carry her purple suitcase down the stairs. It seemed ages since she had arrived and he was sad that she was going, but then he remembered that Peter would soon be moving in next door and he cheered up.

Later, at the airport, Ella was about to leave with the flight attendant who was taking her on to the plane. There was lots of hugging and kissing between Ella and Mrs Thomas, which Jack found embarrassing. He hoped she wouldn't try to hug him. She didn't, but instead just lightly punched his arm.

'It's been great, Jack,' she said.

While Mrs Thomas was sorting out details with the flight attendant, Ella made sure she could not be heard.

'It's good nobody found out about the shelter,' she said. 'We'd just get into all kinds of trouble and we might even be in the papers.'

'I suppose,' said Jack. Then a thought struck him.

'The papers!'

'What about them?' asked Ella.

'I've just remembered,' said Jack. 'I took that newspaper back to 1940, and gave it to Peter. He said he would keep it in his room.'

'So?' asked Ella.

'Well,' said Jack. 'What if Mr Bennett finds it when he's clearing out?'

'What's weird about finding a newspaper?'

'He said his father, Peter, I mean, died a couple of years ago. So won't he get suspicious if he finds a newspaper with last week's date on it?'

'Oh Jack,' laughed Ella. 'You're such a worrier. Even if he does find it, it won't prove anyone went back in time, will it? That will just be our secret.'

'I suppose,' said Jack. 'Bye then.'

'It's been awesome,' said Ella. 'Let's catch up by text!'

Jack and Mrs Thomas waved goodbye as Ella walked away to the plane.

Meanwhile, back in Cotswold Gardens, Mr Bennett was sorting through the last of the things in the house. He found a small suitcase under a bed. Inside were some personal items of his father – Peter. There was a box-brownie camera, a gas mask, and some ration books, and under them was an old, yellowing newspaper.

He took out the items and put them in a box marked 'family history', to be looked at later. He gave the newspaper a quick glance and saw that it was not an interesting old one, but just one dated from a week or so previously. He put it on a pile of other papers and magazines to be burned. It crumbled into pieces as he laid it down.

He carried the pile down to the garden and shoved the whole lot onto the bonfire.

Suddenly a thought struck him. Why on earth had a paper printed last week been in such poor condition? It had looked as if it were 80 years old! And what, he thought, was a newspaper from just a week ago doing in a suitcase in a house that had not been disturbed for years? He rushed over to the bonfire to try to extract the newspaper, but it was too late – the flames had consumed it into a pile of ash.

'Odd,' thought Mr Bennett to himself, then shrugged and went back indoors.

Printed in Great Britain
by Amazon

77007646R00104